Crispens Point

JoHannah Reardon

ISBN: 1475116853
ISBN-13: 978-1475116854

DEDICATION

To my mother, who told me I could do anything and that I was especially good at writing.

CHAPTER ONE

Mrs. Bartholomew's nose twitched as she peeked out the window. All anyone looking at her from the outside would have seen was one eye squinting and half of her nose scrunched up. She loved to watch what was going on in the neighborhood without being detected, as if languishing for the good old days of the cold war, when an enemy could be raking his leaves right across the street.

"She's a pretty little thing, Custer." Custer was her golden cat who kept watch with her in almost as furtive a manner. He purred loudly as if to confer. "I wonder who she is?" When Custer failed to respond, she continued, "She seems to be all alone. That's a twin bed going in now, and I haven't seen a double. No kids, either, because there's no baby furniture or toys. She looks to be about thirty, wouldn't you say?" In answer, Custer stood up and stretched, jumping down from the sofa and mewing loudly to go out.

"You're perfectly right, dear. We need to go meet her. I'm glad I made those cookies yesterday. We'll take half of them over to her. That should encourage her to talk." Mrs. Bartholomew made her way slowly into the kitchen, pulling a basket off of the top shelf. After laying a towel inside, she piled it full of her famous oatmeal chocolate chunk cookies. Custer jumped on the table to get a better view and to make sure there were no bits of chicken or chunks of tuna in the basket.

After arranging it just so, she slipped out of her house shoes and into the pumps she kept by the door. Looking in the mirror hanging at the entrance, she tucked a few grey hairs back into her tidy bun and pinched her cheeks to get some color into them. Custer rubbed back and forth between her legs, anxious now to go out. As she opened the door wide, he dashed out and disappeared into the bushes. "Aren't you coming with me?" she called after him, but Custer had seen a bird and lost all interest in what was happening across the street.

So Mrs. Bartholomew made her way around the moving van and the men who were quickly getting all of the young woman's belongings into the house. She walked up the brick sidewalk and peeked into the open door of the little clapboard bungalow. She'd been in it before, of course, and knew that the living room leaked slightly in a heavy rain. She'd always liked the place, though. Although small, it had lots of what her sister would call charm, from the rustic fireplace to the pine cabinets in the kitchen. Both bedrooms had slanting ceilings and window seats, which gave it a cozy look.

"Hello," she yelled as loudly as her cracked old voice would project. "Can you hear me?" No one answered, so she boldly marched in. "I'm from across the street. Hello." In answer, she heard water running and the mysterious young woman walked out of the kitchen.

"Oh! Who are you?"

"I'm Mrs. Bartholomew, your neighbor across the street. I've brought cookies to welcome you to the neighborhood."

"How thoughtful!" She looked truly pleased as she took the basket from her. "I'm not used to small towns yet. In the city no one would have noticed that I'd moved in."

"You're a city girl then?" Mrs. Bartholomew asked with the savvy of a personal investigator.

"Most recently, yes. I can't believe how quiet and peaceful it is here. That's what drew me to the place."

A large man carrying a chair interrupted. "This is the last of the furniture, Miss. Just boxes left now."

"Thank you, Joe. Put the rest of the boxes in the garage in the back. I'll go through them later."

"Yes, Ma'am," Joe nodded to his associate and headed back to the truck.

The young woman smiled and looked after them. "I'm not used to being called ma'am. Another nicety about country life, I think."

Mrs. Bartholomew squinted at the woman, trying to think what information she needed next. "So what brought you to Crispens Point?"

"Let's go sit down at the kitchen table. I'm exhausted and I want to try one of these cookies."

Mrs. Bartholomew followed her in and sat down in a straight backed chair at an oak table. She approved of the woman's practical choice of furniture. The woman sank into the chair with a sigh and took a bite of a cookie. The look she got on her face reminded Mrs. Bartholomew of Custer when he catches a mouse. "Delicious!" was her only comment, then she suddenly added, "The remoteness and the low cost."

"What?" Mrs. Bartholomew looked at her as if she'd just said that she'd flown in from Mars.

"You asked why I came to Crispens Point. It was because it was country like and the housing market was reasonable. I can't afford city prices."

"I see." Mrs. Bartholomew looked around her for a clue as to what to say next. "There aren't many jobs here. You going to travel into the city?"

"Heaven forbid! I'm planning on becoming a country girl for good."

"You come across an inheritance or something?"

"Oh no. Why would you ask that?"

"I just don't see how you'll make a living here, that's all."

The woman jumped up and filled a paper cup with water. "I need to wash down that cookie. I could eat the whole batch, but I'd regret it later."

She sat back down and sipped her drink. Mrs. Bartholomew looked annoyed. "You'll starve!"

"What? Oh no, one cookie will hold me for now."

Mrs. Bartholomew blew air out of her mouth in exasperation. "No, I mean, you'll starve if you don't have work."

The woman laughed. Mrs. Bartholomew liked her laugh. It sounded like her wind chimes that rang in the wind. "I'm a writer. It doesn't matter where I live. My novels sell well enough to make a comfortable living for me. I'm not rich but I can make the house payment and have enough left over for the necessities."

Mrs. Bartholomew sat up straighter, looking like Custer when he was about to surprise a bird. "What's your name?"

"Charlotte Fyne."

Mrs. Bartholomew looked disappointed as she waved her hand. "I've never heard of you."

Charlotte laughed again, "I suppose not. I've never made the New York Times bestseller list."

"You don't write trashy romances, do you?"

"Never! Only extremely dignified ones." Charlotte smiled realizing she'd found a way to tease her.

Mrs. Bartholomew didn't look convinced, but decided to leave it at that. "You won't be having men drop by all the time will you?" Her eyebrows connected in a frown that served as a warning. To her surprise, Charlotte's mouth turned downward at the corners.

"I'm afraid not. I'm pretty good about writing romance, but I haven't been able to snag a romance of my own. The man I thought I'd marry left me for another a couple of months ago. I haven't had the courage to look further since then."

"Nonsense. We'll have you married off in no time. You're too young and pretty to be all alone like me."

"That's the nicest thing anyone's said to me for weeks. It's been awhile since I felt young or pretty."

"Well, you are." Mrs. Bartholomew nodded her head once as if it were a done deal and no more discussion could be allowed.

"I'm happy the way I am for now. I'm confident that if God wants me married, he'll send the right man in the right time."

Mrs. Bartholomew perked up at the mention of God. "You religious?"

"I don't know if religious is the right word. I love God and want to follow him if that's what you mean."

"Of course I do." She looked put out. "You have a denomination?"

"In the city I went to a nondenominational church. I noticed the Community Church as I drove in, so I thought I'd visit it on Sunday."

"Hrmph. It's kind of a newfangled church." She lifted her chin with frown, looking as if Charlotte had just said she'd go to the races on Sunday.

"I guess I'll have to find out for myself if it's a good fit."

This seemed to mollify Mrs. Bartholomew. She stood up suddenly as if her mission was accomplished and she needed to start a new one. "I'd best get back home."

Charlotte walked her to the door and waved to her when she turned back to look at her from her house. "Thanks again for the cookies."

Mrs. Bartholomew nodded and headed inside with Custer at her heels.

CHAPTER TWO

Charlotte turned to the many boxes that needed to be put away after watching her neighbor disappear inside. She liked this little house a lot better than her apartment in the city, so she didn't mind the work that was ahead of her. And in spite of what she'd just said to Mrs. Bartholomew, she didn't mind living alone. It gave her plenty of time to write, which was her first love.

Five years ago, she'd quit her job as a day care director to pursue writing full time. The one novel she'd worked on for years, finally sold giving her enough of an income to leave the security of her job. Now she had fifteen books on the market, creating enough of a nest egg that she was able to afford this place. At first she'd been nervous about small town life, but the idea had grown on her steadily.

She was putting away her dishes when she heard a knock on the window in the back door. A man in overalls and a baseball cap waved to her as she swung the door open wide. "Yes?"

"Howdy. I knocked on your front door, but you didn't hear me, so I came around back."

Charlotte nodded and waited.

"I'm from the gas company. I just wanted you to know, you're all hooked up."

"Thank you."

"You're welcome." He stood there and smiled, looking pleased with himself as if he'd rescued her from a burning building. "Nice place you have here."

"Yes, it is. Well, I've got a lot to do. Thanks for hooking me up." She started to close the door when he stopped her.

"Since you're new here, I thought you'd like a tour of the town. I'd be glad to show you around."

"Oh, that's okay. I'd rather explore it myself." Charlotte felt bad when his face fell, but it was better to get this over with now. Years of being single had taught her that.

"Here's my number if you change your mind." He handed her a scrap of paper with something scribbled on it.

"Thanks." She closed the door firmly this time and rolled her eyes as she turned away. She finished putting away her dishes and started on the pots and pans when she heard a firm knock on the front door. Still holding a frying pan, she opened it to a man in a three piece suit, holding a briefcase.

"Well, hello! I heard you were new in town, so I popped in to see if you needed any insurance. I sell to everyone in town."

"No thanks. I already have insurance."

"Well, then, how about dinner?"

"Pardon?"

"How about going to dinner?"

Charlotte stared wide-eyed before speaking, "Um, I don't know you."

"Well, dinner is a great way to get to know me."

"Thank you for the offer but I have a lot to do."

"Everyone's got to eat."

"I'll manage."

He stood there a moment more struggling to find another way to convince her, but he finally gave up and walked out to his sports car.

Charlotte went back to the kitchen and had gotten as far as the silverware when she heard a knock on the window above the sink. A man in a Hawaiian shirt stood waving at her and motioning toward the back door. When she opened it, he threw his arms in the air and said, "Whoa! You're as pretty as they all said. I just had to see for myself." He then turned and walked away without another word.

Charlotte shook her head and grinned, thinking, "This town must be in desperate need of women. I wonder if any of them send off for mail order brides." Then a second thought occurred to her. "What will Mrs. Bartholomew think after I assured her no men would be stopping by?" In another hour she finished the kitchen without further interruptions and decided to make a grocery store run for supplies.

She got in her car and drove to the one and only food market in town. It was about half the size of the store she was used to shopping at, but the food looked fresh. Her cart was getting full when a woman with bright red hair, dressed in a pastel flowered blouse tucked into a sky blue skirt, stopped her. "Are you Charlotte Fyne?"

"Yes, I am."

"I love your books! I heard you were moving into town."

"My, news travels fast."

"Oh yes, everyone knows everything about you. Your realtor told us you were coming."

"So, you know where I live?"

She nodded her head and her red curls bobbed up and down. "The old Fowler place. That's a cute house. I thought it would sell fast." When Charlotte didn't respond, she added shyly, "If I brought lunch over tomorrow, would you mind signing one of your books for me?"

"I'd be glad to. You don't have to bring lunch."

"No, I want to. It'd be an honor."

"Okay. I'd like that. What's your name?"

"Janice Powers. I work as a teller at First National Bank."

"It's nice to meet you, Janice. We'll see you tomorrow then."

Charlotte left the store feeling glad that a woman instead of a man wanted to get to know her. There was something about Janice she liked. Maybe it was her bright demeanor or her warm manner. At least she explained the men showing up one after the other at her house. News had obviously spread that a romance writer was in town.

Janice showed up right at noon the next day carrying a basket of sandwiches, fruit and fresh vegetables. With Mrs. Bartholomew's cookies, it was a perfect lunch. "I can't believe I'm having lunch with Charlotte Fyne. I've read all of your books. My favorite is *Love Falls*, which I've read three times. It's the one I brought for you to sign."

"Why don't I do it right now before we forget?"

Janice handed her the book. "I'll bet you get tired of doing this."

"I've only done it at book signings. You're the first person to recognize me in my normal life. It's kind of fun."

"Are you kidding? I figured you had the most glamorous life possible."

"No, my life is actually very sedate. I'm alone a lot without much adventure. I guess that's why I write stories. It makes my life more interesting."

"So you've never married?"

"I'm afraid not. I'm still looking for Mr. Right. How about you?"

"Me too. I'm beginning to think he doesn't exist." Her red curls drooped and bright blue eyes dimmed at the proclamation. As quickly as that mood had come upon her, it fled as she asked, "Tell me what your perfect man would be like."

"Oh my goodness, you'd think I'd know that with all the writing I do about it." Charlotte rubbed her forehead and looked into the distance as if she were seeing a vision. "First of all, he has to be a Christian, and not just someone who says he's a Christian. He has to follow God with his whole heart and his life should reflect Jesus Christ in his actions. Second, he needs to be pursuing goals he feels passionate about. If I'm going to follow this man around, I'll need to be confident that his goals are big enough to absorb my interest and participation. Third, I have to like being with him." She paused a moment then added, "I guess that pretty well sums him up. Know anyone?"

Janice laughed, reminding Charlotte of Lucille Ball, "If I knew someone like that, I'd nab him for myself."

They finished their lunch and Charlotte saw Janice to the door. She noticed Mrs. Bartholomew standing slightly behind one of the bushes across the street, so she waved to her. Mrs. Bartholomew jumped as if shot by a BB gun, since she thought she was well hidden. She tried to act like she was pulling weeds and waved to Charlotte. She definitely had to work on her detective abilities with this woman in the neighborhood. She had a feeling Charlotte would be much more interesting than old Mr. Fowler who used to live there.

Charlotte went back inside, surveying her small domain. Everything was in its place except her office, which would take a while. She began going through her manuscripts, skimming through some of her favorite parts. There were times she felt like she couldn't write at all and going back to read her successes helped to re-inspire her. She was now working on a novel about a woman who met her love on a trip to the South Pacific. "Maybe that's my problem," she thought. "I never go anywhere, and now I've moved to this minuscule town. I don't suppose I have a chance of meeting anyone here. Oh well, at least three men are interested in me. And delightful fellows they are!"

The day went quickly and Sunday arrived before she knew it. She'd been looking forward to Sunday quite a bit because she knew that a lot of her social life would revolve around the church. She put on her most conservative clothes since the rumors were flying around town about her. It's best to counteract my reputation right away, she thought as she chose a tan skirt with a navy blue blouse, low heels, and very little make-up. When she was convinced that she was properly school marmish enough, she headed out the door, walking to the church which was just a few blocks down the street.

Stepping into Community Church, she liked it at once. A sunny building with lots of windows, it had been a Congregational Church years ago which folded and became an antique store, but was now reclaimed for its original purpose. She saw with pleasure the warm wood of the pews inside and the worn beams that lined the ceiling of the sanctuary

Immediately she was accosted by numerous people. "Welcome, Charlotte. We're so glad you could come today," and "Janice told us you'd be coming. Would you like me to show you around?" plus her favorite by a young man, "Gee, I didn't know romance authors went to church." By the fifth person, this notoriety was wearing thin. She just wanted to sit down and become anonymous.

Finally battling her way through the crowd, she found a spot in a side pew about half way back. Out of the corner of her eye she saw Janice on the other side of the church and waved discreetly. She could see a couple of elderly women in front of her look at her furtively then whisper to each other

She was saved when a piano and guitar began playing instrumental music which focused everyone on the front rather than on her. She bowed her head and prayed that they would all be able to worship instead of check each other out. Just when she was feeling that her heart was prepared, the minister stood up to make announcements and she lost her focus. He was about average height, had a deep, strong voice and dark brown eyes that sparkled with excitement. Most people would call him nice looking but Charlotte thought he was beautiful. She couldn't help staring at him, but would scold herself for such ungodly thoughts about the pastor. After a few minutes, she composed her wild imaginings and remembered why she was in church. These kinds of mental images couldn't be good. He gave a good sermon about living as if the invisible kingdom were visible. She liked it a lot.

When church was over, she once again was surrounded by a small fan club, but the minister paid no attention to her whatsoever which was just as well. Janice left her parents and sister and moseyed her way over to Charlotte. "Well, what did you think?"

"It was great. Even better than I expected. I think I've found a church home."

Janice then leaned in and whispered, "What did you think of Pastor Gordon?"

Charlotte blushed which annoyed her no end, "I liked his sermon very much."

"He's a great teacher," she nodded. "And he's single, but don't get any ideas. He's a confirmed bachelor. Many women around town have already tried."

Her words made Charlotte almost choke. She had to get out of there. The last thing she wanted was to be seen as the romance writer who was after the pastor. She would avoid the man at all costs. After saying her goodbyes, she escaped out the front doors and almost ran home. She didn't even wave to Mrs. Bartholomew who was just arriving home frustrated because everyone at her church already knew about Charlotte.

CHAPTER THREE

Pastor Gordon McCrae pulled off his tie and collapsed into his easy chair. He turned on a baseball game and put his feet up. After Sunday morning, he usually popped a dinner in the microwave and fell asleep in his chair, but today his mind wouldn't stop. He'd been invited over to the Johnson's house for Sunday dinner, a frequent event since he was single. Many of his parishioners felt sorry for him and fed him often. They constantly tried to set him up with one of the local girls, or a distant cousin who was visiting from another state, but he fended off their attempts gallantly. In spite of their insistence, he liked being single. He liked being able to come home after church and turn the ball game on, come and go when he wanted, and have plenty of time to study. As attractive as the opposite sex was, the whole prospect of a relationship scared him. Mostly women talked a lot more than he was willing to listen, and the emotions they displayed in his counseling office made him feel like running and hiding. No, he didn't care how cute the prospects were, he'd rather stay as he was.

But today Charlotte Fyne had showed up in his church. He knew she was coming to town, of course, but someone as different as a romance writer coming to Crispens Point would set the tongues wagging for weeks. He'd heard the rumors along with everyone else, but thought he'd be able to avoid her like the plague until he saw her sitting in the side pew. He knew it was her right away, even before all the whispers swirling around him confirmed it. The rumors were that Charlotte was pretty. He'd heard Mrs. Folsom, the realtor, say that she had a dark complexion and hazel eyes, was rather on the small side, and had a habit of twirling her auburn hair with her finger when she was nervous. That's what had given her away when he glanced at her. She was twirling her hair like crazy.

Normally such an observation would have caused him to chuckle, but wouldn't catch his attention any other way. But there was something about Charlotte. After that first glance, he consciously looked away from her. Even when he looked toward that side of his congregation, he purposely fixed his gaze toward the back of the row so that he wouldn't see her. He noticed her briefly as she slipped out of the church when it was over. She avoided him as actively as he avoided her, which annoyed him for some reason that he couldn't explain.

And here he was, sitting in his arm chair, thinking about her again. He particularly liked the way her nose turned up at the end, making her look like she was an imp about to get into all sorts of trouble. As soon as that thought went through his mind, it sobered him up. She was a romance writer, for heaven's sake. He'd given whole sermons about how romance was out of control in society and the need to look at each other through God's eyes rather than our ridiculous notions about knights in shining armor or beautiful princesses about to emerge from the crowd. He'd never read a romance, nor would he consider it. He could hardly stand to sit through a movie where someone kissed somebody. In fact, he'd given a few sermons about that too. Well, there was just one thing to do. Avoid being near that woman as if she had leprosy.

Just as he was getting his thoughts under control by concentrating on the baseball game, the phone rang. It was Mrs. Donahue. "Pastor, I'm sorry to bother you,"—Gordon noticed that everyone said that when they knew perfectly well that they were bothering him and weren't sorry a bit—"but I'm planning on having some people over for dinner this Friday night. Would you like to come?"

"Sure, Mrs. Donahue, you're the best cook in town. Would you like me to bring something?"

"Oh no, just yourself. We'll see you around six o'clock then."

Gordon hung up the phone with a smile on his face. Mrs. Donahue was like a mother to him and her husband made a great ping pong companion. No one knew from week to week who would win since they were so evenly matched. He relaxed at their house more than any other place.

As soon as she hung up the phone with Pastor Gordon, Mrs. Donahue dialed Charlotte. "Hello, this is Mrs. Donahue. I met you at church this morning. My son was the goofy one that said he didn't know romance writers went to church."

"Oh yes, I remember you." Charlotte smiled as she recollected the boy's face. She'd liked the woman very much.

"Oh good, I was hoping you would. I was wondering if you would like to come over for dinner this Friday night. We're having a few people over from church."

"That sounds lovely. What can I bring?"

"Not a thing."

"Are you sure? I make a really nice seven layer salad."

"Okay, if you'd like to bring that, it would be perfect with lasagna. Will six o'clock work for you?"

"That would be fine. Where do you live?"

"Just around the corner from you on Lyon Street, number two fifty-four."

"Great. See you then."

Charlotte got off the phone and sat back down at her laptop where she'd been typing furiously. The call was good for her. She'd been losing herself in an imaginary world since she'd gotten home from church. It had forced Pastor Gordon's brown eyes out of her memory and had given her all sorts of energy to write. Her editor would be thrilled. At this rate, she'd finish before her deadline. The call reminded her of the real world she lived in and renewed her desire to get to know the people of her new church.

In the meantime, Mrs. Donahue called Janice since she knew her to be a friend of Charlotte's, and the Colton family who had a boy the same age as her son, Mort. After inviting them all, she turned to her husband, "What did you think of Charlotte today?"

"Can't really say. Just met her for a minute." He was annoyed when his wife asked him questions like that. He mostly wanted to get back to the Western he was reading.

She ignored his obvious attempts to shut her out. "What about her and Gordon? What do you think?"

He jerked his head up, "Now Martha. Don't get any ideas. Gordon's a big boy and can take care of himself."

"Well, he's not doing a very good job at it so far. He's been here for three years and he hasn't found anyone. I think he needs my help."

"Absolutely not. If I hear a word about you pushing those two together, I'll throw a fit. I mean it."

She smiled to herself as she turned away. She knew in spite of his threats that he'd not say a thing. He was the mellowest husband this side of the Mississippi and she loved him for it. She really did feel a responsibility to take care of Gordon. All her own kids were married, except for Mort who wouldn't be old enough to think of such things for years. Ever since Gordon had come, she'd paired him off with different women in her mind, but nothing had come of it. She knew there wasn't much she could do other than create an environment for something to happen, so Friday night was a good start.

CHAPTER FOUR

After the phone call, Charlotte looked out her front window and noticed Mrs. Bartholomew working in her garden. She felt a sudden compulsion to go help her. The woman looked lonely. She put on her old shoes and dug out some worn gloves and went across the street to join her.

Custer ran up to her as soon as she set foot in the yard, meowing a greeting, or warning; Charlotte wasn't sure. "Hello, Mrs. Bartholomew! Could you use some help?"

Mrs. Bartholomew straightened her back and squinted into the sun as Charlotte approached. All the enthusiasm she'd felt yesterday disintegrated when she realized everyone in the town knew more about Charlotte than she did. "Oh, hello. I'm just pulling weeds." She didn't even smile. Why bother?

"I'd love to pull weeds. I actually know a bit about plants. My mother is an avid gardener. And it's such a beautiful day. I need an excuse to be outside."

Mrs. Bartholomew looked her over as if seeing her through new eyes. After a moment of silence, she said, "Very well, why don't you work on the beans over there? They have lots of thistles growing by them."

Charlotte looked at the prickly plants and was glad she'd thought to bring her gloves. She set to work, trying to visit as she pulled. "So, tell me about yourself. Have you lived in Crispens Point your whole life?"

Mrs. Bartholomew straightened her back and pulled a sleeve across her brow. "Yes, I have. My husband was a farmer, but after he died I sold the farm and bought this little place. The proceeds from the sale gave me enough to live on. Never had any kids so had to let the old place go. It'd been in my husband's family for years." After saying this, she looked off into the distance as if seeing another place and time.

"That must have been awful."

Mrs. Bartholomew snapped back to the present with a look of disgust. "No more awful than most people. I've had a good life. Nothing to complain about." She went back to work and the conversation lagged. Charlotte wondered why she was so silent today compared to yesterday.

"Is gardening your main hobby?"

"I don't know if you'd call it a hobby. More like a necessity. I like to eat fresh foods but don't like to pay grocery store prices."

"So what do you like to do?"

"I don't know." She looked annoyed at having to answer such a question and they fell silent again. After a few minutes, she added, "I like to paint."

Charlotte looked up with interest. "What kind of painting?"

"Oils."

"When we're done here, will you show me some of them?"

Mrs. Bartholomew nodded and they continued on with a smattering of conversation as they worked. Custer romped between them, batting the weeds around when they threw them. He seemed pleased about all the activity around him. At long last, Mrs. Bartholomew stood up and pulled off her gloves. "Well, let's go inside then."

Charlotte gladly stood up and brushed herself off, following Mrs. Bartholomew into the house. As soon as she stepped through the door, she blinked in astonishment. There were paintings everywhere. On the walls, displayed on easels, tiny ones on tables, it looked like an art gallery. She was immediately drawn to a large one over the fire place. It was a garden scene with brightly colored blooms bursting out at every angle. It reminded her of the book *The Secret Garden*, which she'd read as a child. "This is extraordinary. Where is this?"

Mrs. Bartholomew walked up next to her and smiled. "That's my wildflower garden I had at the farm. I could see it out of my kitchen window when I did dishes. It looked just like that, framed in my window. I painted it exactly like my view when I knew I'd have to sell the farm."

"Oh, that makes me even sadder about you having to leave, but what a wonderful way to preserve the memory." Charlotte then turned her attention to the other works of art around her. All of them were of a country scene of some kind, from rickety old bridges to broken down sheds. She loved them all, but after a while she noticed that none of them contained a human. There was something rather sad about that.

"Would you like a glass of iced tea?"

"I'd love one."

Mrs. Bartholomew disappeared into the kitchen and came back with two tall glasses. They settled onto her living room sofa that looked as if it had been purchased at least twenty-five years ago. It was still in perfect shape, in spite of the outdated design. Charlotte sipped her tea and asked, "Have you been painting all your life?"

"No." She shook her head as if it were a silly question. "I used to doodle all the time, but didn't know I could paint. It wasn't until after Harold died that I started. Took an art class offered at the community center, taught by a professor from the university in Carlston. Then I started painting as if my life depended on it."

"Therapy." Charlotte said nodding her head.

"What?"

"The painting was therapy since you'd lost your husband."

Mrs. Bartholomew wrinkled up her nose as if she smelled a skunk, "I don't know about that nonsense, but I know I liked doing it. It was a way to preserve everything I loved. I don't know what will happen to it all when I'm gone."

"Have you ever tried selling any of it?"

"No! That would be like selling my babies. I painted them for me. No one else would care a hoot about them."

"I don't know. I think they're quite good."

"Well, I'm not selling them." Her expression looked as steely as if Charlotte had suggested selling Custer.

Charlotte smiled to try to ease the tension. "Of course not. I don't blame you."

Mrs. Bartholomew visibly relaxed and decided she liked this new neighbor. "What did you think of Community Church?"

"I liked it. The people were friendly and the music and sermon were good."

A thought seemed to occur to Mrs. Bartholomew, "Nice looking pastor too."

Charlotte blushed as if she'd been accused of adultery and choked on her sip of iced tea. "I guess so," she responded as casually as she possibly could, but Mrs. Bartholomew smiled broadly. She finally knew something no one else in town knew yet. Charlotte was sweet on the pastor.

CHAPTER FIVE

Monday morning arrived overcast and misty. Charlotte reluctantly put aside her novel for a few hours to accomplish all the necessary things involved in a move. She put on her yellow slicker with matching yellow boots and set out into the dreary day, doing her best to brighten it. Her first stop was First National Bank since that's where Janice worked. She ran inside and pulled off her hood, noticing Janice right away. "Hi. How are you?"

Janice had been punching numbers madly, but she looked up with a frown at Charlotte's greeting. As soon as she saw who it was, she grinned, "Hello, Charlotte. I'm fine. I just can't get this balance figured out. What's up?"

"I'm here to open an account. Can you help me?"

"No, I'm just a teller. But Barbara will be glad to fix you up. She's over there." Janice pointed to a woman talking on the phone at a nearby desk. "Just sit down and wait until she hangs up."

Charlotte nodded and sat down on the green vinyl chair just as Barbara hung up the phone. "Well, hello. How can I help you?"

"I need to open a couple of accounts."

"Okay. What's your name?"

"Charlotte Fyne."

The woman looked up sharply and glanced at Janice, who smiled back at her. "Ohhh," she said, as if a great mystery had been solved. "You're the romance writer."

Charlotte nodded, annoyed at this label being slapped on her again. One of these days she was going to figure out a witty response.

"I've never read any of your books. Are they pretty steamy?"

Charlotte felt every bone in her body sag. She was so tired of this question. Somehow she pulled herself together to answer cheerfully, "Not at all. They're what you would call a sweet romance." She smiled a particularly sweet smile as if to demonstrate, which seemed to cause Barbara to lose all interest in her or her books. From that point on, it was all business.

Finishing with that, Charlotte stopped back by the counter to see Janice. "Are you doing anything for lunch today? My treat if you'd like to eat out."

"That would be great. I brought my lunch, but it's only peanut butter and jelly. It'll keep until tomorrow."

"Where do you suggest?"

"How about The Junction? It's an old railway station that's been done over. They have great sandwiches."

"Sounds perfect. I'll see you there at noon?"

"I'll be there." She bobbed her curls and showed her dimples. Her dress had bright flowers spattered all over it, making her look like a blossom unfolding in the middle of the somber bank. Charlotte liked her a lot.

Next on her stop was the hardware store to pick up odds and ends for a few small repairs and some paint for the bedroom. Charlotte was pleased with herself that she could manage pretty well with most of her household projects. Unless it involved plumbing or carpentry, she did all her own work on the house. She enjoyed picking out a sky blue for her bedroom. It was presently a dirty shade of cream. Evidently Mr. Fowler hadn't spent any time on redecorating. She'd decided to do a room a month and her bedroom was first on her list.

"Excuse me, could you mix this color for me?" Charlotte handed the man behind the counter a slip of paper that was a dreamy shade of blue. She'd seen the color on a wall in a magazine and cut it out to match it. "Sure. No problem. We've got one of those newfangled machines that reads the color. We can match anything."

He took the slip over by the paints and attached it to a computer. After reading the numbers it displayed on the screen, he began to add drops of color to the white base. While the paint was being shaken to smithereens on the mixer he asked, "You live around here?"

"Yes, I bought the old Fowler place."

"Ooh," he said as he grinned and hung his head like a shy boy who's trying to get up the nerve to look a girl in the eye for the first time. A moment ago, they had conversed like old friends, but now he felt awkward. Charlotte rolled her eyes and walked away to look for the other items she needed when out from the back the man who had looked through her kitchen window burst through the door. He had on the same Hawaiian shirt. Carrying a long piece of lumber, he almost rammed into her. "Sorry." When he saw who she was, he set the wood down with a thump. "Oh, it's you. Hey, Wilbur, it's the romance lady. Ain't she as pretty as I said?" Wilbur, who was pounding the lid back onto her paint can, just grinned and nodded. He'd become mute.

Suddenly Charlotte had enough. Her eyes narrowed and she put her hands on her hips. "I'm not the romance lady.

I happen to write books about people who fall in love. I'd appreciate it if you'd not call me that."

Wilbur gave a hiccuppy kind of laugh and the Hawaiian shirt hung his head. "I didn't mean nothin' by it. Don't get all mad." His little boyish manner mollified Charlotte, but she gathered the rest of her stuff together and escaped as soon as possible.

By this time it was eleven thirty, so she decided to head over to The Junction to wait for Janice. She ordered a coke and sipped on it as she read a book she kept in her purse for moments such as these. As usual, when she read, the time flew so she was surprised when Janice walked in what seemed like a few minutes later.

"Wow, it feels good to sit down," Janice proclaimed as she flopped into the booth. "So what do you think of this place?"

"It's cute. I like how they kept the feel of the old train station."

"Yea, they did a good job. It's actually a distant cousin of mine who runs it. I'm kind of proud of that."

"You should be."

"So how's life treating you so far in Crispens Point?"

Charlotte sighed and looked at Janice for a minute, trying to decide whether to be honest or not. She felt she could trust her. "I like the town a lot, but I'm fighting all the preconceived ideas about what I'm like because I'm a romance author. You'd think a hooker has come to town by the remarks I've been getting."

Janice giggled and nodded. "I guess that's true. I'm sorry everyone's making all these judgments before they get to know you. The notoriety will wear off in time. You have to be patient with us. Any newcomer causes a stir and you're as close to a celebrity as we've had."

Charlotte gave Janice a small smile, just barely turning up the corners of her mouth. It was unconvincing so Janice added, "Would it help if I threw a party to introduce you? That way people could get their curiosity satisfied, and they would see that you're just a normal person. Besides, I like any excuse for a party."

Charlotte looked at Janice more kindly this time. She was impressed with her. "You are really sweet to offer such a thing. I don't know what to say."

"Say yes! How about a week from Saturday?"

"I guess that would be fine. But only if you let me help."

"Agreed." Janice took a bite of the sandwich that the waitress had brought her. She loved the reubens here although she knew all that fatty corned beef wasn't good for her. "Do you miss your friends from the city?"

To Janice's surprise, Charlotte's eyes teared up. She dabbed at them quickly with her napkin. "I'm sorry. I don't mean to be such a baby. It's just that..."

Janice moved her hand over Charlotte's to reassure her, "What is it, Honey? You can tell me."

And Charlotte thought she could. She hadn't talked to anyone about it since it happened, so she took a deep breath and started in. "I was engaged to a man who I thought was perfect for me. When he asked me to marry him, I knew I was the luckiest woman in the world. Then last year, he began growing more aloof. I thought maybe it was because we were getting married so he was concentrating on other things rather than pursuing me. But suddenly, a few months ago he broke our engagement. He'd met another woman at work and knew that she was the one.

"That was bad enough but he also took all my friends with him. I'd only lived in the city for a few years and met him right away, so all my friends were his friends. He left me with no one."

Janice leaned over and squeezed her hand again. "What a jerk! How could someone leave a woman as sweet as you?"

Charlotte laughed, changing her countenance in every way, "Very easily, evidently. I started looking for a place to settle down right after that which brought me here, so I'm starting over. But I know one thing. I will not give my heart away quickly again. Maybe God wants me to stay single."

"That's kind of ironic considering what He's given you to do, don't you think?"

"Oh, I don't know. Jane Austin was single her whole life and she wrote the best romances ever. Who knows? Maybe if I married, I'd lose my edge. Besides, I'm getting pretty set in my ways."

Janice shook her head from side to side, sending her red curls flying. "Not me. I'd throw everything about my life away for a good man. I just can't seem to find him. When Pastor Gordon came, I thought he was the one for sure, but winning him over is like trying to thaw out a snowman in Alaska. He has about as much romance in his body as a turtle."

Charlotte laughed but somehow felt sad about this information. However, the good thing was that it gave her one more reason to avoid Gordon McCrae.

CHAPTER SIX

The week flew by. Charlotte finished several more chapters in her novel. Mrs. Bartholomew put some completing touches on a painting, canned some pickles, crocheted a baby sweater for the pregnancy center, and gave Custer his weekly bath to which he protested so loudly that Charlotte could hear him howling from across the street.

Wednesday night arrived and Charlotte decided to attend a Bible study on the book of Romans that Pastor Gordon was teaching at church. This took some courage on her part because she knew it would be a smaller group than on Sunday morning, but she couldn't live in fear of running into this man. She'd just put all foolish thoughts of him out of her mind and look to him as the teacher that he was. It would also be good if she could be around him without getting all fluttery inside, which would take practice, so she might as well start now.

She took out her well worn Bible and put it in a satchel with a notebook and a pen. Once again, she dressed in her most conservative clothes, blue polo and khakis, and pulled her hair back into a pony tail. She put on small pearl earrings as her only jewelry. She would convince these people that she was a decent person! Walking down the block, her confidence grew as she neared the church that had guitar music drifting out to the street through the open doors.

Once inside, Janice accosted her immediately. "I'm so glad you've come. We aren't very many on Wednesday nights, and I've always wished for a friend. Will you sit with me?"

"I'd love to." Charlotte started for the sanctuary which was all lit up.

"Oh no, not in there. That's worship practice. We meet in the fellowship hall. There are usually only about a dozen of us."

Charlotte stopped walking and felt like bolting out the door. Only a dozen? It would be pretty hard to be anonymous in that group. Janice noticed that she'd stopped and turned around to look at her. "What's wrong?"

Charlotte knew that she couldn't possibly explain, so she shrugged her shoulders and walked ahead. "Nothing, I just think I'll duck into the bathroom real quick. I'll meet you there, okay?"

"Sure, I'll save you a seat."

Charlotte almost ran to the bathroom. Once inside she looked in the mirror. Sure enough, her face was bright red again. For being dark complected, she sure blushed easily. She splashed some cool water on her face and patted it dry, trying not to rub off her make up. Taking a few deep breaths, she prayed, "God, help me here. Take my mind off the pastor and onto You. I don't want to be this way." With a last look in the mirror, she stepped out into the hallway. Following the sound of voices, she went into the fellowship hall.

Fortunately Pastor Gordon had his back to her, so she didn't have to face him right away. She thought she was all through blushing now so she slipped quietly past him and sat next to Janice. She turned to speak to her right away so she didn't notice that Pastor Gordon's face tensed when she sat down. No one else noticed either.

After a few more people trickled in, he cleared his throat. "Welcome, everyone. I'm glad you all could make it. Well, let's get started. We're on Romans, chapter five."

A woman on his left raised her hand right away. "Wait, Pastor. Aren't you going to introduce the new person?" She fairly bounced in her seat in anticipation.

Pastor Gordon was extremely annoyed, but he tried not to show it in his words or actions. "Well, Louise. I'm afraid I can't do that because I haven't met her myself. Janice, is this a friend of yours?"

Janice beamed at the attention. "Why yes, she is. This is Charlotte Fyne. She's just moved to Crispens Point. I've only known her a few days, but I already love her."

Charlotte smiled and made eye contact with everyone except Pastor Gordon. No one seemed to notice that he also avoided looking at her. "With introductions finished, let's open in prayer." With that he bowed his head and prayed eloquently about God's holiness. The regular people thought it was a more heartfelt prayer than he usually said. Charlotte thought it was a powerful prayer which took her right into God's presence.

They opened to Romans 5 and began to read God's word together. Pastor Gordon gave them some background information and then had them read the first eleven verses together. As he asked questions, the group came alive in their discussion. Charlotte mostly listened, hesitant to speak when she was so new, but she couldn't keep quiet when they got to verse three about how we are to rejoice in our sufferings. She'd been learning about this first hand. "How in the world are we supposed to do this?" he asked, and the room grew silent. Finally Charlotte blurted out, "We do it because we believe that God has a plan. That He knows better than we do what is best for our lives; that suffering leads to perseverance, character, and hope like it says in verse four. We do it because we trust Him."

Pastor Gordon looked up with a start when Charlotte began to speak. He'd almost forgotten she was in the room, but now her presence loomed large, as if she were three times her normal size. Her answer was perfect, but for some reason he couldn't acknowledge it so he simply said, "Yes, any other thoughts on this?"

"It's pretty hard to beat that answer, Pastor," said Harold who was sitting on the other side of Charlotte. "I think she summed it up pretty well." Everyone else nodded and Pastor Gordon affirmed them. "You bet. It was a good answer. Let's go to the next question."

The study went smoothly after that. Charlotte was pleased with herself that she didn't say anything silly or inappropriate. She even looked directly at Pastor Gordon as long as he didn't look at her. If his eyes caught hers, they both looked away quickly. He made her heart flutter when she studied him without his knowledge, but if he caught her gaze, she felt her heart do a cartwheel. She felt confident that her inner response would get better with practice.

Pastor Gordon, on the other hand, felt even more frustrated. Each time he saw her profile, he caught himself studying her. He purposely ignored her the rest of time unless she made a comment, and then he went on to other things immediately. He didn't like her being in his Bible study. He didn't like it a bit.

Friday evening arrived determinedly, and Charlotte prepared to go to the Donahue's. She decided to walk since they were just around the bend. For the first time, she dressed up a little more, feeling secure enough to get rid of her matronly look. She put on a peasant blouse and a nicely fitted pair of jeans. With her hair curled and a new bracelet on her wrist, she even dared to put on some perfume. Feeling satisfied with a last look in the mirror, she stepped outside into the beautiful evening. She was pleased with how her salad had turned out too, so she carried it in front of her with confidence.

Because it was such balmy weather, the neighborhood was out in full force. Mrs. Bartholomew waved from her front porch, with Custer alert on her lap. She secretly wondered where Charlotte was going all dolled up, but felt it against her principles to ask. So instead she watched her walk down the street and then tip toed through Charlotte's back yard to catch a glimpse of where she was going. Charlotte turned back to look at one point, but Mrs. Bartholomew thought she was well hidden behind the big oak. She finally lost interest when Charlotte turned into Donahue's driveway. There was nothing important happening after all. She'd just turned around when she noticed the car across the street. It was the pastor's car from the Community Church. She had a good eye for color and his car was an unusual shade of green. She'd noticed it before and was sure of it now. Things were interesting after all. She wished she could be Custer for a while and sneak into a window well to watch.

If she had been in a window well, she would have seen plenty. Charlotte arrived at about the same time as

Janice. They chatted for a minute then rang the doorbell. When Mrs. Donahue opened it, she welcomed them with open arms. Charlotte smiled broadly until she walked in and saw Pastor Gordon sitting there. He had his head bowed and resolutely refused to look up. Charlotte felt her face go bright red and wished she'd worn her tans and blues, anything other than a peasant blouse and perfume. To make matters worse, Mrs. Donahue made a big deal of Charlotte's arrival. No one noticed Mr. Donahue's eyes roll in exasperation. "Look, Gordon, have you met Charlotte?" She smiled and held Charlotte's arm as if she were the queen of England, displayed for all to see.

Pastor Gordon looked up and gave a brief smile. "Yes, we've met."

"Oh, I'm glad. She's going to be one of your parishioners, you know."

Gordon nodded and turned back to talk to Mr. Donahue. Charlotte felt horribly on display, so changed the subject to what she should do with her salad. Mrs. Donahue looked disappointed but led her into the kitchen.

Gordon continued to converse with Mr. Donahue on the latest rise in wheat prices, but inside he was going crazy. How could the Donahues do this to him? What was going on? Was this some kind of test from God? If so, by gum, he'd pass it.

"What can I do to help, Mrs. Donahue?"

"Oh, nothing dear. Go on in with Janice and Gordon. They're better company than me."

"That's all right. I'd rather stay in here and help."

Mrs. Donahue sighed, but handed Charlotte a knife to begin cutting the French bread. "So are you adjusting well to small town life?"

"I think so. I'm not quite used to how well everyone knows everyone else. That's taking some getting used to."

"I suppose it does. That's the way it's always been so I never think anything of it." She leaned over to watch Charlotte's progress. "Here's some butter and garlic salt. When you get the loaf cut, just butter and salt it."

"Okay. The lasagna smells wonderful. Italian food is my favorite."

"Good! I'll go fill the water glasses." She disappeared with a pitcher in her hand. Just then the door bell rang and Charlotte heard new voices. It gave her relief to know that more were coming. At that moment, Mort came flying through the kitchen. When he saw her, he stopped cold. "Oh hi! Mom said you were coming. Romance writers can cook too?" He grinned and rushed on to greet his friend. By this time, he knew perfectly well that he was being ridiculous. Charlotte liked him, though. She could take that kind of teasing.

Soon Mrs. Donahue was back dragging Charlotte out of the kitchen. "I want you to meet the Coltons. This is John, Cindy, and their son, Trevor." Looking at them she said, "And this is Charlotte, our beautiful new neighbor." She looked directly at Gordon when she said this, but only her husband noticed. "Have a seat, all of you. I'll be done in just a minute."

They all shared peripheral information when dinner was announced. Mrs. Donahue not only produced a fantastic meal, but decorated the table with several living plants and stamped place cards with each of their names. Charlotte was horrified to realize she was seated next to Gordon, but relieved that he ignored the names and sat down with a space between them, quickly switching Janice's name tag with his own. Mrs. Donahue looked confused when she came into the room and saw the seating arrangement, but there wasn't much she could do about it at this point.

Dinner proceeded quite nicely with lots of pleasant conversation, laughter, and teasing. Charlotte kept quiet most of the time and observed. Pastor Gordon turned out to be a great story teller, keeping them entertained with one tale after another. Janice also kept the conversation lively, giving the boys something silly to talk about every few minutes.

When they'd all eaten enough to take care of a herd of elephants, they pushed back from the table and wandered into the living room for coffee. The boys drifted off to their own affairs and the adults continued in polite conversation. Finally Mrs. Donahue announced that they were going to play a game. "This is a little different than most parlor games, but it's a great way to get to know each other." She said this as she passed out pieces of paper and pencils to each guest. "Write on your paper the word 'people', and then list five of the people that are dearest to you in the world." She gave them a few minutes, then added, "Now write the word 'beliefs', and list the five beliefs that you feel you can't live without." Pausing a bit while her guests tapped their pencils and looked off into the distance, she concluded, "Now write 'activities' and list your five favorites." After a minute more Mrs. Donahue asked, "Everyone done?"

After several nods, she said, "Cross off three of the people on that list. Leave only two."

"Wait a minute," said Cindy. "Why just two? How am I to pick?"

"That's up to you, just do it." After several grumbles, each person complied. "Anyone want to share which two they left and why?"

Janice piped up first. "I crossed off my neighbor and my cousin. I couldn't decide between my mom, dad and sister, though. I left three because I couldn't choose."

Mrs. Donahue shook her finger at her. "That's cheating. Did anyone do it right?"

"I have two because I crossed off my brother and two sisters and left my parents. It seemed the easy way to do it but I have no idea why." Pastor Gordon shrugged his shoulders.

"Hmm. Well, at least you followed the rules. Anyone else?"

Cindy refused to answer, but John said he'd crossed off his parents and sister and left his wife and son.

"What about you, Charlotte?"

Charlotte looked embarrassed. "I just have one left: my mom."

"Why only one?"

Charlotte shifted in her seat, wishing she didn't have to answer. "I had a lot of acquaintances on the list but only one is really dear to me, my mom, so rather than choose between the others, I just chose her."

Mrs. Donahue looked sad for a moment, but kept the party spirit going. "Let's move to activities." The next two things didn't seem as hard to do as choosing between people, and lots of laughs occurred during the discussion of activities. Charlotte easily pared all three categories down to one, her mom, her writing and Jesus Christ. Other than that, the rest were all peripheral. Everyone seemed a little jealous of her ability to do this, but the whole exercise made Charlotte blue.

When the evening ended, everyone headed home laughing and in good spirits, but as soon as she was out of the door, Charlotte felt the weight of the evening, wishing she had more of value in her life to vie for first position. As Pastor Gordon saw her walking home in the dark, he felt the same sadness for her. He wanted very much to offer to walk her home, but squelched the thought as soon as it entered his mind. Instead he got in his car and drove a block away, watching to make sure she got back to her house safely.

CHAPTER SEVEN

Gordon McCrae woke up crabby as could be on Saturday morning. He felt annoyed enough to kick a dog. Fortunately there were none around so the canine world was safe.

He'd tossed and turned all night, fighting images of Charlotte invading his dreams. In one, she held a bouquet of flowers that turned into a shining knife. That's exactly the way he felt about her. She seemed everything attractive but could only be deadly to him. He felt the dream somehow prophetic, although he'd never had any confidence in his dreams until now.

His sermon tomorrow was on I Peter, chapter three, concerning wives and their husbands. He really resented having to preach on this text, even having to think about it, but that was the next thing in I Peter, so it was pretty hard to avoid. And, of course, he knew there were plenty of married people in his congregation who needed to hear what Peter had to say, so he sat down to work on the verses.

When he got to the part in verse three about how beauty should not come from the outside but from the inside, he felt like he was preaching it to Charlotte alone. She needed to see how all this romance stuff was ungodly, and that she should concentrate on her character instead. Suddenly this verse became the central theme of the sermon and he pounded away at it. He practiced it over and over until his voice thundered throughout the parsonage. He could hardly wait until tomorrow.

Charlotte woke up happy. She was going to paint her bedroom today. She already saw how the blue paint would transform the room, making her feel like she was looking at the open sky. After eating a bite of breakfast, she covered the furniture with plastic and taped around the windows and floor boards. Soon she was painting to the sound of music flowing through her little house. She danced and thought and sang at the top of her lungs. Something about doing a mindless activity like painting released all her creative juices.

Through the music, she heard a pounding on her door. When she answered it, there stood Janice in old jeans and a bedraggled t-shirt. "Hi. You told me you were going to paint today, so I'm here to help."

"Bless you, child. Come on in. The paint is fresh."

"Ooh, I love the color. Where should I start?"

"How about that side? We'll meet in the middle."

The two of them now sang, danced, and conversed together, giggling like two school girls. With both of them working, they finished at about one o'clock, all except for a little trim work, so they sat down in Charlotte's kitchen and ate a tuna sandwich. "That was a lot of fun last night," Janice said as she nibbled.

"Yes, it was."

Taking a bite of sandwich she added, "I've always had a crush on Pastor Gordon. Isn't he dreamy?"

Charlotte frowned, "I don't know if dreamy is the right word. He's more like Gregory Peck in *To Kill a Mockingbird*, always dignified and trying to do the right thing."

Janice nodded, "That's what I mean, dreamy." She smiled mischievously, like an elf about to pull a chair out from under you. "To me, that's what dreamy is. You can have all those goofy guys who do anything for a laugh. I want a man with courage and dignity."

Charlotte nodded without enthusiasm, but Janice didn't seem to notice. "Did you see how Pastor switched the name tags last night?"

"Yes, I did notice that..."

"I'm afraid to hope, but I wondered if he wanted me on his right side instead of his left."

"I don't know. Has he shown any interest in you?"

Janice sighed, looking like she'd lost her best nickel. "No, not a bit. But then again, he never shows interest in any one. I think the man's made of steel." She looked up at Charlotte with a gleam in her eye. "I thought maybe you would crack his shell, but if you are, he's not showing any signs of it."

Charlotte laughed a little too hysterically, "Get that idea out of your head right now. He has absolutely no interest in me. I might as well be invisible."

Janice suddenly perked up, "Do you want him to notice?"

"No!" Charlotte almost shouted. "Not at all. I want a warm man who is understanding. I don't think that's Pastor Gordon."

Janice laughed and seemed convinced, which set them both to parroting his mannerisms and speech. Charlotte felt a bit guilty about it but enjoyed it all the same.

Sunday morning dawned and Charlotte got ready for church without any qualms. She'd slept on the sofa last night since her room smelled strongly of paint, but she enjoyed walking into the bedroom and seeing all that fresh blue color. She got ready in record time and decided to head to church early. Sometimes she liked to be in there praying before all the hustle and bustle started. That way she could also avoid all the conversation that swirled around her ahead of time.

Walking into church, she saw only a few people seated. Most in attendance were involved in some aspect of the service and milled around taking care of details. Charlotte made her way to the same spot she'd chosen last week and opened her Bible to read. After a chapter or two, she began to read some hymns, causing her heart to sing long before the music began up front. Finally she noticed that the church was filling up and sweet melodies began drifting out to the congregation.

After a lot of singing, some announcements, and time of prayer, Pastor Gordon got up to speak. He had a strong voice and commanded everyone's attention. "The passage we are looking at today is in I Peter, chapter three. Turn with me, if you will." Pages shuffled as everyone tried to find the verses he would speak on. "God gives clear instruction here concerning husbands and wives." From there he expounded on the text sharing how wives were to win their husbands over by their behavior.

Charlotte nodded in agreement, enjoying the truth to be found in these passages. When Pastor Gordon reached verse three, his voice rose the way a storm rises over the ocean. "Clearly our society has not taken this verse to heart: 'Your beauty should not come from outward adornment, such as braided hair and the wearing of gold jewelry and fine clothes. Instead it should be that of your inner self, the unfading beauty of a gentle and quiet spirit, which is of great worth in God's sight.'

“Think of the millions of dollars that women spend on themselves to look attractive for men. Both sexes are at fault here; the women who put so much emphasis on their looks and the men who encourage it." At this point Pastor Gordon looked directly at Charlotte. "And there are those who actually make their living by encouraging these things. Instead we, as Christians, should set the example by putting the emphasis on our inner spirits. We need to wake up!" He said this with such force that the light fixtures overhead shook.

Although he looked at Charlotte to strike conviction in her heart, he was disconcerted by the fact that she was smiling and nodding her head the entire time. And in fact, Charlotte did agree with every word. Not for one moment did it occur to her that he was talking about her occupation. He didn't know that her books demonstrated inner beauty over outer, that her passion in writing romance was that women would recognize this very thing.

Somehow, the fact that she smiled made Pastor all the more vehement in the way he delivered his sermon. Being new, she thought that this was a typical way for him to preach. If she'd looked around, however, she would have noticed the wide eyes of the rest of the congregation. As it turned out, people would talk about this sermon for weeks.

When church was over, Charlotte decided the direct approach was best. She couldn't continue to duck and hide from the pastor if she was going to come each Sunday. Besides, she really liked his sermon and wanted to tell him so. Marching up to him, she thrust out her hand, gripping his firmly, "That was very powerful, Pastor. A much needed message for all of us." Her grip was firm, but his was rather limp, an oddity for him. He didn't smile when she did and felt certain that she was mocking him, that her whole reason for coming to his church was to mock him. He'd never met a woman like her who could haunt his thoughts.

So Charlotte left the church in high spirits leaving Gordon's spirit in shambles.

As she walked toward her house, she saw the insurance salesman standing next to his corvette, looking impatient. Her first impulse was to turn around and go the other way, but she really wanted to go home. She took a deep breath and marched confidently up to him. "Selling insurance on Sunday? Don't you ever rest?"

He looked startled to hear her voice; he hadn't noticed her walking up. "Oh, no. I'm not selling anything today. This is purely a social call."

Charlotte walked around him, heading resolutely for her door. "You just sit around waiting in women's driveways?"

He laughed, "I never have before, but that's how badly I wanted to meet you. I felt like we got off on the wrong foot the other day."

Charlotte turned around to look at him, placing one hand on her hip in annoyance. "We didn't get off on any foot. I don't know you."

He hung his head, looking like a school boy whose companions had run off and left him. It was rather endearing. "I know. That's what I mean." He lifted his head and stuck out his arm, "I'm Frank Rubin, a local boy who has tried to make good."

Charlotte felt like a heel but she refused to take his hand. "And why should I care about any of that, Frank Rubin?"

"Good question. Exactly." He answered, relieved that she hadn't sent him away. "There is no reason you should care. That's why I was hoping I could take you to lunch. Maybe you'll find me worth knowing." He grinned, showing dimples, reminding Charlotte of her cousin, Joey.

Everything in her told her she should just turn around and walk into her house, but the house seemed so lonely, that she hesitated. "I know you just came from church," he continued. "I go to First Church on Elm Street. Our service got out a few minutes before yours." He looked at her hopefully, like a little boy waiting to be rewarded with a lollipop for being good. "I thought it might be important for you to know that."

Charlotte studied him a minute, trying to figure him out. "Okay, Mr. Rubin. Where would you like to go for lunch?"

"Really? Great! How about we drive over to Carlston? There's a steak place there I'll bet you'll love."

She stepped down into his corvette and settled into the bucket seat. “What am I doing,” she thought. “I don't know anything about this guy.” But there was something about him she liked and trusted. She wished she'd put this off so she could ask Janice about him, though.

They sped off into the country side and Charlotte had to admit she liked zooming along in this attractive little vehicle. She rolled the window down and he yelled out landmarks of interest as they traveled onward. They arrived in Carlston about twenty minutes later, as he ran around to her side to open the car door. So far, he'd been a perfect gentleman in every way.

The restaurant turned out to be delightful. The decor was pleasant and the food was some of the best that Charlotte had tasted. Frank turned out to be a great conversationalist and she had to admit that she enjoyed every minute of the afternoon.

When he brought her back to her home, he once again opened the door for her and walked her to her front door. She didn't invite him in, nor did he seem to expect her to.

"Uh, Charlotte, this was really nice. Do you think we could do it again sometime?"

"I had a great time, Frank. But I need to process this now. Is that all right?"

"Sure. Absolutely. Take all the time you need. I'll ask again, don't worry." He smiled his little boy smile, looking content with the world.

"Thank you." She unlocked her door and slipped inside, waving one last time to Frank who was now getting back into his car. She sat down on her sofa, ignoring the paint smell that still permeated the house. "He was nice," she said out loud. Living alone had caused her to talk aloud more than she used to. "I like him. But he doesn't seem to have much spiritual depth, even if he does go to church. Maybe I've made too big of a deal out of that and no one will ever live up to my expectations." She picked up a pillow and traced the floral design with her finger, thinking unwillingly about Pastor Gordon. "I think I need to talk to Janice about this."

CHAPTER EIGHT

It was several days before the opportunity to talk to Janice presented itself. She invited her over for lunch, making a quiche, a fruit salad and some oatmeal cookies. The house smelled good when Janice walked in the door. "Mmm, am I hungry! I can't wait to taste what you've made." She was dressed in bright yellow today, looking like a daffodil in full bloom.

"I think you'll like it. It's a recipe that I've used for years."

They settled into the kitchen chairs and Janice admired the fresh flowers on her table. "Thank you. They're from Mrs. Bartholomew across the street. She's a dear, even if she is a little nosy."

"I don't really know her, but I've never seen her without that cat at her heels. He must be at least fifteen years old."

"Yes, Custer is quite loyal. Sometimes I think he gives her information the way she's always consulting him."

Janice bit into the quiche and gave a purr of satisfaction, sounding quite a bit like Custer when he's rubbed behind the ears. They settled into casual conversation until Charlotte felt she could ask her a more personal question. "What do you know about Frank Rubin?"

"Frank, well..." She rubbed her chin and looked like she was concentrating. "He's a Crispens Point boy, has always lived here. Made quite a success at the insurance business with customers all over the county. He banks with us so I've seen his account balance. It's pretty impressive." She looked at Charlotte, trying to figure out what this was about. "Is that what you want to know?"

"Not really. Actually, he told me more or less the same. I want to know more about his personal life."

Janice's eyebrows shot up, making her look more startled than she felt. "Why the sudden interest in Frank?"

Charlotte bit her lip, looking like a school child who's just been caught passing notes. "He took me out for lunch on Sunday. We had a nice time, but I realize I don't know anything about him other than outside information. I was hoping you could fill me in on inside stuff."

Janice nodded. "I can tell you plenty. Probably way more than you want to know. Can I have another cup of coffee before I get into this?"

"Sure." Charlotte poured and Janice began. "Frank was a real jerk in high school, one of those athletes who was full of himself, thought he was God's gift to women, all that kind of attitude." She took a sip and Charlotte waited patiently. "But when he graduated, he sort of fell through the cracks, got in trouble with the law, and had to do a stint in the Army or go to jail. It turned out to be the best thing for him. The Army taught him discipline, which he applied to selling insurance when he came back to Crispens Point. Can I have another one of those cookies?" Janice was easily distracted by food. Charlotte shoved the plate toward her and waited. After taking a big bite and swallowing, she continued. "He married Shari, his high school sweetheart, probably the most popular girl in high school. The trouble was that she was as self-centered as he was and hadn't learned discipline through the army, so she divorced him after a couple of years. I always felt kind of sorry for him because I think he really wanted to make a go of it. Anyway, Frank's okay. I approve of him."

Charlotte sat silently stirring her coffee. She'd added way too much cream and stirred it now in hopes that some of it would evaporate. "What's he like spiritually?"

"Oh, I'd say he's a Christian, faithful churchgoer, volunteers for charitable events and stuff. I've never actually had a conversation with him about that, but I've always seen him as a sheep rather than a goat. Even in high school, he stood up for what he believed in, which didn't carry a whole lot of weight because of his lifestyle, but I wouldn't hold that against him now." Janice took her last bite of cookie then asked, "Do you like him?"

"Yes, I do like him. I don't see how someone could not like him. He's very pleasant."

"But..."

"I don't know. There's just something missing."

"Well, I'd date him if he asked me, but he's never even looked my way." Janice patted her red curls as if they were to blame for her failed social life. Charlotte stared at her a moment more and wondered why someone hadn't snapped her up years ago. She was adorable.

"Thanks, Janice. I value your opinion more than I can say."

"Wow, that's really nice. I don't think anyone's ever told me that before, except maybe my little sister. I never dreamed when I first read one of your novels that I'd ever sit in your kitchen and talk about men. It makes me believe anything can happen!"

Charlotte smiled and Janice jumped, "Oh my goodness, I'd no idea so much time had gone by. I've got to get back to work. Thanks for the food and the fellowship."

Charlotte walked her to the door and waved as she climbed into her car. Mrs. Bartholomew's cat sat in the window watching and Charlotte thought for a moment that she saw the woman herself peeking out, but she couldn't be sure. Just in case, she waved over that way. Inside her house, Mrs. Bartholomew jumped.

Gordon McCrae was happy. After the frustration he felt Sunday, he went on a long run and felt much better. He'd gotten that woman out of his mind and hadn't thought of her again all week. He knew he'd probably see her tonight at Bible study, but he was prepared. The thought of her being there didn't bother him at all. He knew who he was and she couldn't change that. He'd decided that if her presence bothered him, he'd just pretend she wasn't there. He thought it would work.

Besides, the passage they were studying tonight was complicated. He doubted very much that she'd be able to contribute, so it should be easy to ignore her. He felt so good that he whistled all the way to church, and continued humming when he got inside.

Sure enough, right on time, Charlotte walked into the room, once again sitting by Janice. The other people in the study seemed glad to see her which was fine for him because no one noticed his inattentiveness. In fact, he was still humming as he turned to the second section of Romans 5.

Everyone participated at the beginning when they were talking about Adam and Christ and the similarities and differences. Charlotte kept quiet during this discussion which really pleased Gordon. However, toward the end of the study, it grew quieter and quieter as each person tried to figure out the relationship between sin increasing and grace increasing all the more. Pastor Gordon started to worry a little about how to help his people understand the concept, but he kept stumbling over how to explain it. Finally Charlotte interrupted in her soft, gentle voice. "Pastor, isn't it just a matter of understanding that we are sinners and desperately need the grace of God? The more we comprehend our sin, the greater we understand God's great kindness to accept us through Christ. Until we know for sure what big sinners we are, we can never know how much we've been forgiven."

"Oh, I see. It's quite simple when you put it that way," said a man on her left.

"Yea, I get it now," added a woman. "Thanks, Charlotte."

"You oughtta consult her when you get stuck, Pastor," another man said.

Pastor Gordon turned bright red, but before he could say anything Charlotte added, "Not at all. Pastor knows a million times more than I do. I just happen to be able to put things in words easily."

Pastor Gordon nodded, "Thank you. Well, that wraps up the study. Any questions?"

There were a few which he answered coherently to his supreme joy, then they closed in prayer. As they were walking out, Charlotte approached him, “I hope I didn’t embarrass you, Pastor. I never meant to.”

“Not at all.” He wasn’t sure where to go from here. He didn’t really want to continue the conversation at all, but it was hard to avoid. “Do you have any Bible training?”

“Oh no. I just have been in lots of Bible studies and love to read it and study it on my own. I don’t really know very much.”

At that moment Janice caught up with them, “Pastor Gordon, I’m having a party on Saturday night for Charlotte. Won’t you come?”

Gordon started to shake his head “no” when a chorus of voices who’d overheard said, “You’ve got to come, Pastor. You can pray for her as we welcome her to our community.” “That’s right, besides if you’re there, lots more people will come.” “I’ll stop by and pick you up, Pastor,” added a young man. Gordon didn’t know what to do so he nodded in agreement. He didn’t feel like humming when he left church that night, but he thought maybe he’d misjudged Charlotte.

As Pastor Gordon got ready to go to the party, he began to smile. He had to admit he sort of liked this girl. He’d been fighting the attraction that he’d felt toward her but maybe he didn’t have to. Maybe she was all right and he’d been so much on his guard that he hadn’t been able to recognize her true character. For the first time in ages, he put on a little cologne and spent a little more time than usual on deciding what to wear.

Arriving a little late to the party, he was amazed at how many people were there. Janice had decided to use her parent's house since it was bigger than her apartment, and although their living room was large, almost every nook and cranny was filled with people. Evidently Charlotte's fame had spread like wildfire and curiosity brought out Crispens Point in droves. After all, the last exciting thing that happened here was when Ralph Morris' barn burned down.

He caught a glimpse of Charlotte talking in the kitchen and his heart leapt at the sight of her. He realized now that his heart had been doing that from the beginning, but he'd been so careful that he'd ignored his feelings. His impulse was to run right up to her but he didn't want to be obvious. After all, he had no idea what she thought of him. So instead, he began to visit with those around him, glancing her way every now and then.

Finally, enough time had gone by that he felt he could approach her to converse. His hands began sweating and he noticed he was clenching his teeth. It had been a long time since he'd felt this way. Something about it made him feel almost giddy, like a little kid going to the circus for the first time. He'd almost reached her, when Frank Rubin stepped in front of him. "Hi Charlotte, I'm sorry I'm late. I had a customer that I couldn't shake. How have you been since I saw you last?"

Charlotte gave him a warm smile and reached her out to give his hand a squeeze. "I've been fine, Frank. It's wonderful to see you again. I missed you."

Frank beamed and Charlotte beamed back. Pastor Gordon's face fell and he turned quickly to retreat. He moved so fast through the room that he bumped into a few people. One of them asked, "Are you okay, Pastor? You don't look so good."

"I'm not feeling too well. Would you tell Janice I had to head home? It's a big day tomorrow, after all."

"Sure. I hope you'll be all right."

Gordon nodded and shot out into the cool night air. "How could I be so stupid!" he yelled once he was a good distance from the house.

CHAPTER NINE

Pastor Gordon recovered quite nicely from the previous evening. His sermon was composed and sensible. No one could have known what he went through. After the party he'd gone home, read his Bible, and drifted into a dreamless sleep, waking Sunday morning as if he'd never met Charlotte Fyne.

He felt released from her too. When he saw her at church, he smiled in a friendly manner, feeling victorious that it hadn't hurt a bit. He was able to treat her as anyone who was coming to his church and wish her the best spiritually, without being entangled emotionally. It felt wonderful. He confirmed again that he was meant to be a bachelor, and glad for it.

Charlotte, of course, had no idea what had been going on in his mind, and she thought that for the first time he acted as if she really existed. It was nice.

She'd enjoyed the party that Janice gave her. Most of the names had already escaped her, but she still felt the warmth of such an enthusiastic welcome. She'd greeted Frank more warmly than she'd meant to, but she really was happy to see him. They'd agreed to another lunch date today.

He picked her up at church when the service was over since she'd walked there. Pastor Gordon noticed her get in Frank's car and drive away. He was happy for her.

Charlotte arrived home later in the afternoon feeling tired. It had been a big weekend and she wanted nothing more than to put her feet up. She'd just turned on the TV when the phone rang, "Hello, little girl, it's your mother."

"Hi, Mom. It's good to hear your voice."

"How's small town living?"

"It's taking some getting used to, but I think I'm going to like it."

"I'm taking next week off. Mind if I visit?"

"Oh, that would be wonderful. I'd love it. Maybe you can give me some decorating ideas, and I want you to see my neighbor's garden. You'll be impressed."

"I'll get there tomorrow around noon. You know me, always the early riser."

"I do indeed. I'll have lunch waiting."

Charlotte hung up the phone feeling satisfied. Something about her mother coming to visit made everything seem right. They'd fought like badgers when Charlotte was a teenager, but now they got along like best friends. Charlotte's mother had learned that rare ability of knowing when to quit giving her opinion.

The day her mother arrived, the sun shone and the birds chirped their welcome. She got out of her car and stretched. Mrs. Bartholomew noticed the stranger, of course, and wondered who she could be. She never guessed it was Charlotte's mother, because they looked nothing alike. Charlotte was rather small and curvy. Her mother was tall and thin. Their complexions were completely different too. Charlotte's was dark and tan; her mother as pale as Snow White. Only their hair seemed similar.

Mother walked to the front door and knocked quickly before walking in. "Charlotte, it's me."

"Mother! How was your trip?" She leaned toward her and embraced her, kissing her on the cheek.

"Great. The weather couldn't have been more cooperative." She pulled back and looked around her. "Good choice, Charlotte. This place is delightful."

"I thought you'd like it. I'm pretty pleased with it myself."

"I'm here to work as well as visit, you know. Any painting or wall papering, I'm available. I also do a pretty good job of stenciling."

"Thanks, Mom. I'll try not to work you too hard."

They sat down to lunch after putting Mother's things in the guest bedroom. "So, Darling, have you met any eligible young men yet?"

"Mother! I've only been here two weeks."

"I know, but at your age, you can't wait forever. Better get out there and snatch up the good ones right away." She ginned and Charlotte knew she was teasing, but the trouble was she felt the same urgency.

"I have met one guy."

"I thought so. I noticed that gleam in your eye."

"He's an insurance salesman. How boring is that?"

"There could be worse things. At least it's legal." They both laughed and Charlotte felt the warmth and understanding between them. "So, is this serious?"

"No, not at all. I enjoy being with him, but I'm not sure he's what I want. I'm trying to figure that out now before I get in too deep."

"Wise girl. So when do I get to meet him?"

"Actually, I've invited him over for dinner Friday night. We'll see how he enjoys spending the evening with my mother. That should tell a lot about him."

Janice joined them for dinner that night, and she and Mom got on like a house afire. Mom felt especially happy that Charlotte had found a friend so quickly. She'd worried about her a lot when Charlotte's boyfriend left her suddenly, but Charlotte proved herself stronger than Mom thought.

She also met Mrs. Bartholomew. They talked gardens for hours. In fact, Charlotte was afraid she wasn't going to get her mom back again, but eventually she returned and they got to work on wallpapering her kitchen. The great thing about working on projects with her mom was that the conversation flowed the whole time. They hadn't spent time together in months because of both their schedules, but they made up for it now. Charlotte respected her mother's opinion more than anyone's.

Because of that, she was very anxious for her to meet Frank. She needed to find out what her mother truly thought. Because of that, she didn't tell Frank that her mother would be there. She didn't want him to reschedule.

Wednesday night, Charlotte took her mom to Bible study. Everyone greeted her like a member of their own family, including Pastor Gordon. Mom liked them all and got a lot out of the study. "That pastor's a good teacher, Charlotte. Nice looking too."

Charlotte looked at her mom as if she'd pinch her, "Stop it, mother. You get to meet Frank. Be happy with that."

"Okay, okay. I can't help it if I have eyes," and she grinned a little too knowingly.

Friday night finally came. Charlotte planned a simple meal of baked mostaccioli, salad, and bread sticks, with peppermint ice cream for dessert. Frank arrived right on time, bringing a box of chocolates and flowers, impressing Mom right away. "Hi Charlotte. These are for you. Sweets and beauty for the sweet and beautiful."

"Thank you. They're lovely. Frank, before I put them in water, I want you to meet my mother. She's staying with me this week."

"Mrs. Fyne, it's a pleasure to meet you. Your daughter has spoken of you very fondly, a rare thing these days between mothers and daughters."

"Oh call me Margaret. Mrs. Fyne makes me feel ancient."

"Margaret, it is."

The two of them sat down on the sofa while Charlotte retreated to the kitchen. “So tell me, Frank, what’s the best thing about Crispens Point since I hear you’re a life-long resident.”

“The best thing... I’d say it’s the way everyone cares about their neighbor. When I was in the service, I realized for the first time what a great place this was. I returned as soon as possible and have no intention of leaving.”

Charlotte came back into the room and Frank stood back up. “Can I help with anything?”

She waved her hand, “No, I’ve got it under control. The mostaccioli just needs a few more minutes.” She handed each of them a tall glass of iced tea and slipped into the chair on the other side of the room. Frank and Margaret returned to their conversation and Charlotte sat contentedly listening to them banter. By the end of the evening they acted as if they’d known each other for years.

When the evening ended, Charlotte walked Frank out to the car. “Thanks for including my mom so much in the conversation.”

“Are you kidding? She’s great. If my mom were that interesting, I’d love it. I’m really glad she was here.” He reached up and brushed the back of his hand against her cheek. He wanted to do a whole lot more, but knew he’d have to take it slow with Charlotte. It was worth it, though. She smiled and grabbed his hand, squeezing it as she turned to go back into the house.

"Well, Mom, what did you think?"

"I thought he was delightful. More to the point, what do you think?"

"I like him. I don't know him that well. It's only been two weeks. I'm awfully afraid of getting hurt again."

"I know, Darling, but you can't live your life being afraid. It's better to take the chance."

"That's a fine thing coming from you, who's been single since Dad died."

"Ah, but I found the perfect one. Anything else would be a step down." She smiled sadly and Charlotte loved her more than ever.

CHAPTER TEN

As Janice got ready for work Friday morning, she thought about Frank. She hadn't thought of him for years since she had a big crush on him in high school. Of course, everyone had a crush on him in high school. But back then, he'd had eyes only for Shari. There was something that bothered her about him being paired up with Charlotte. She wasn't sure what it was, but it nagged at her.

Janice was tired of being single. She'd moved out of her parent's house a couple of years ago, which made her feel more independent. But she'd been a lot lonelier since then. She missed the good natured bantering that went on in a family and longed to start her own. She'd even tossed around the idea of adopting an unwanted child just so she could have her own family. But, she felt her motives were wrong in wanting to adopt for herself and not for the child, so she dismissed the idea.

Her mood had perked up since Charlotte came to town. She believed that they connected so quickly because she already knew a lot of Charlotte's thoughts from her novels. Why Charlotte attached herself to her, she wasn't sure but was thankful for it. She hadn't had a best friend since high school and Charlotte was the best one ever.

Maybe that's why the thing with Frank bothered her. She'd just found this great friend, and he was going to take her away. Not away, just monopolize her attention. She knew she was being petty, but she couldn't shake the feeling just the same.

The thought did occur to her that she was jealous that Charlotte had been here just two weeks and already was dating someone. Janice hadn't dated anyone steadily for years. She'd thought of subscribing to one of those dating services, had even filled out a form, but in the end she couldn't make herself turn it in.

That's why suddenly she'd noticed Victor Mason. Victor had been two grades ahead of her at school. She remembered him as a shy, studious sort back then, even made valedictorian, but no one really knew him. He'd gone away to college and out of the minds of everyone in Crispens Point, but last month he came back. He showed up in church, just about a week before Charlotte came. Janice didn't even recognize him at first until some of the older women began murmuring about him. That got her to thinking about him.

He was rather a mystery. The word was that he married a girl from college, but that she had died of breast cancer. Since he was left with a little girl, he'd moved back home to Crispens Point so that his mother could watch her during the day. He worked as a professor at a university almost an hour away. It was a long commute, but worth it to him.

Janice had never spoken two words together to Victor in high school. She'd tried smiling at him a few times but he never smiled back, so that was the end of her effort. But there was something so tragic about him now. He sat in church with his little girl, looking like the life had been sucked out of him. Janice wanted to help somehow, so she did the boldest thing she'd ever done in her life. She invited him over for dinner. She hadn't told anyone, not even Charlotte. She wanted to write the evening off as a disaster if she had to and not have to explain it to anyone else.

She was rather amazed that Victor accepted her invitation. He'd looked at her a minute, then nodded, murmuring, "What can I bring?", the standard Crispens Point answer, but she'd assured him she'd take care of everything. That comment seemed to perk him up. Perhaps he felt so weary that even bringing a dish to someone's house sounded enormous.

So tonight was the night. She'd put a meal in the crock pot so that dinner would be well on its way when she arrived home after work. Taking one last look in the mirror, she said out loud, "Wow, Janice. Is that a wrinkle? You'd better quit messing around." Then added to God, "Help me not to do anything stupid tonight. Make it what You want it to be."

Just saying that aloud helped her, and she closed the door behind her with a slam.

Charlotte called Janice Saturday morning, "Hi, it's me. Mom just left and I'm depressed. Want to go for coffee or something?"

"That sounds great. I have a lot to tell you."

Charlotte's curiosity rose, "Let's meet at The Junction at ten o'clock."

"Okay, see you then."

By the time Charlotte got there, Janice was on her second cup of coffee and acting like she'd had two espressos. Her eyes were bright, and she almost bounced on her seat. Charlotte slid into the booth. "Okay, lady, tell me what's going on. You look like you're running away to join the circus."

Janice grinned, showing both dimples. Reaching over to grab Charlotte's hand, she said, "I think I'm in love."

Charlotte's eyes got wide, doubt flooding her face. "You're in love?" She enunciated this as if Janice had said that she was an alien.

Janice's smile got even larger, if that was possible, and she nodded her head up and down so hard it looked like she'd get whiplash.

Charlotte's eyes now squinted as if trying to see Janice for the first time. "How can you possibly be in love? I just talked to you three days ago."

"I know. That's what's so crazy about it."

"Crazy is right. Who is the world is this guy?"

"Victor Mason." Janice said his name as if she'd just said Rudolph Valentino.

"Who?"

Now she looked annoyed. "Victor Mason from church. You know, he came to Bible study for the first time last week."

"Oh," said Charlotte as light dawned on her face. "The one whose wife died?" Janice still grinned and nodded as if Charlotte had said something cheerful. "Janice, you hardly know him. How can you be in love?"

"Well... I had him over for dinner last night."

"What? You didn't tell me you were going to do that."

Janice looked sheepish, even a little guilty. "I know. I was afraid to tell anyone. If it had been awful, I didn't want to have to talk about it. But it was wonderful, and I'm in love."

Charlotte hadn't smiled yet and still didn't feel like it. For being a romance writer, she was very cynical about romance. "You aren't in love, Janice. You can't possibly be in love after one dinner."

"But that's what's so amazing. I am." She sat there looking satisfied as if no further explanation were needed.

Charlotte sighed loud enough for half of the people in the restaurant to hear. "Okay, slow down. Tell me why you think you're in love."

"Because I've never felt this way before."

If Charlotte could have, she would have shaken her at this point. "What way, Janice?" She said this as if her teeth were clenched together. Janice didn't appear to notice.

"Like this is the man I want to spend the rest of my life with. Like he's the one I've been waiting for all these years. Like there's never been any other guy in the whole world." As Janice made each proclamation, she raised her voice a little louder and gave a little more emphasis each time. Several people turned around to glance at her, which caused her to lower her voice to a whisper. "He's my dream man, Charlotte."

Charlotte just shook her head, the way an adult would shake their head at a child who consistently made up fantastic stories. "Why is he your dream man, Janice?" This time she said it as if she were weary beyond measure.

Janice looked up at the ceiling as if seeing Victor's face engraved there, "He's kind, gentle, smart, crazy about his little daughter, and loves God. He's dependable, actually has a decent sense of humor, and he likes The Three Stooges. He's perfect."

"Nobody's perfect, Janice."

"Oh, I know, Charlotte. But I think he's as close to perfect as I'm ever going to come."

Something about the way Janice said that, made Charlotte relax. "What does he think of you?"

"That's the best part. I mean, all evening I'm falling head over heels in love with this guy and I'm wondering what in the world he's thinking. But when the evening was over, he invited me to go with him and his daughter to the zoo next Saturday." She smiled so big that you'd think he'd just proposed to her.

"Well, that's nice, Janice, but it's hardly a commitment for life."

Janice waved her hand and laughed. "Oh I know that, but it's a good start, don't you think?"

"Yes, it's a good start. I think I'd feel better if you talked about it that way. All this 'in love' talk is driving me crazy."

Janice frowned for the first time. "Don't you feel that way, just a little bit, about Frank?"

"No, I don't. I mean he's nice. I like to spend time with him, but being in love... I'm not even close to feeling that way."

"Oh well, I guess it's different for everyone. Hey, maybe we can double date."

For the first time Charlotte smiled, "I'd like that." Janice noticed Charlotte was twirling her hair with her finger, and she couldn't understand what was making her nervous.

"Okay, out with it. What's really bothering you?"

"How long has Victor's wife been gone? Are you sure you're not a rebound?"

Janice looked like someone had sicced their dog on her. "She's only been dead a year. We talked about her a lot, but I think that's enough time, don't you?"

Charlotte felt bad because she'd robbed Janice of her joy, making her look miserable in contrast. "Oh, it probably is. I don't know anything about these things. I just think it's something you should keep in mind."

Janice nodded, but she started sipping her coffee slower and an awkward silence settled between them. “Well, I’d better get back home. I’ve got a million things to do.” She started to get up, making Charlotte feel retched, so she grabbed her hand. “When do you want to do this double date?” She smiled so big that her eyes squinted almost shut, trying to counteract her spoil sport words. It worked. Janice perked up. “How about a week from Friday? I’d better not schedule two things for one weekend.” The grin was back in full force, giving Charlotte relief. “Great. I’ll tell Frank. We’ll talk details later.”

Janice nodded and fairly skipped out of the restaurant. Charlotte watched her with a smile on her face. She hoped this would turn out good for Janice. The thought of her getting hurt made Charlotte feel horrible. There was something disconcerting about how sure Janice was about Victor. Charlotte hadn’t been that sure even about John, the man she’d intended to marry.

CHAPTER ELEVEN

Mrs. Bartholomew was confused. She'd been absolutely certain that Charlotte had fallen for the pastor at the Community Church, but now she was regularly seen in Frank Rubin's company. "It's gone far enough, Custer." Custer looked at her through one eye, making a great effort to lift his head on this lazy Saturday afternoon. "I'm just going to have to investigate this matter directly."

She'd noticed that Charlotte had moved her writing instrument—she thought it was called a lap computer or something like that—outside to write under the big shade tree. It was a warm day, so she decided that Charlotte could use a nice cool lemonade. Going to her refrigerator, she poured the pink liquid into a large glass filled with ice cubes. After she made another one for herself, she headed out the door. "You coming, Custer?" Custer didn't even raise his head, so she took that as a "no."

She walked across the street briskly and smiled when Charlotte noticed her and waved. "Here you go. Cold lemonade to take away the heat of the day."

"Thank you. How did you know this is just what I wanted? I've got a folding chair on the porch. I'll get it for you." She stood up, and Mrs. Bartholomew nodded her approval.

When she returned and both had taken a long sip of lemonade, Mrs. Bartholomew asked, "You writing one of them romance novels?"

"Yes, I am. I get tired of being shut inside all day, so I try to bring my laptop outside whenever the weather permits."

Mrs. Bartholomew knew exactly what she wanted to ask next but it'd be too nosy, so she found another way around the matter. "In those books you write, does the heroine always know when she finds her Prince Charming?"

"Not always right away, that's for sure. My Prince Charmings are very flawed, like men in the real world, so it may take some sorting out just as in real life."

"But..." and here Mrs. Bartholomew struggled. "Does your character ever pick the wrong fellow?"

Charlotte laughed. "Not by the end. It wouldn't be much of a romance if she got stuck with the wrong one. That is the ending of way too many romances in real life. No one wants to read about it."

Mrs. Bartholomew nodded looking back towards her house, wishing Custer had followed her out. This conversation wasn't getting her anywhere. She needed inspiration. Finally, she decided on the direct approach. "I've noticed Frank Rubin stopping by."

Charlotte gave a small smile, not at all surprised by the question. In fact, she'd been amazed that she hadn't asked sooner. "Yes. He's been attentive. I've enjoyed getting to know him."

Mrs. Bartholomew nodded and took another sip of lemonade. After a few moments of silence she asked suddenly, "So, still enjoying the sermons at the Community Church?"

Charlotte blushed bright red and Mrs. Bartholomew thought "aha" inside, although her outward countenance remained the same. "Yes, I like them very much. Pastor Gordon is a knowledgeable man."

Mrs. Bartholomew nodded again. She then changed the subject and they discussed Charlotte's mother, her garden, and even Custer. At last she felt enough topics had been covered to disguise her mission. "Well, I'd best let you get back to work. It's been nice talking to you."

Charlotte handed her the now empty glass. "Thanks for the lemonade and the company. I enjoyed it."

Mrs. Bartholomew stepped into her living room. "It's just as I thought, Custer. She's definitely in love with the pastor. I don't know what all this stuff with Frank Rubin is about." She shook her head and walked into the kitchen. Custer stretched and settled back down for another nap.

Charlotte put her head down and began to type, but after a few minutes she stopped. Something in her conversation with Mrs. Bartholomew had disturbed her. She wasn't sure which part it was since they'd conversed about a lot of subjects for quite a while, but after she left she felt a vague dissatisfaction. She decided to go inside and call Frank. Maybe he'd like to do something tonight. She knew they'd just been together last night, but that was with her mother. The two of them could go to a movie over at Carlston.

She dialed his number, but after four rings, she just got the answering machine. She left a message that he should call her and hung up the phone disappointed. She needed a distraction right now.

Walking into the kitchen, she noticed the church bulletin from the week before sitting on her table. Picking it up, she saw there was a bake sale going on this afternoon to raise money for the youth group. She decided to drop by to see if there were any goodies she couldn't live without.

Entering the church, the first person she saw was Mrs. Donahue. "Hi. Are you helping out today?"

"Yes, my husband and I work with the youth group. It was my idea to organize the sale. Look at all the wonderful things people made." Charlotte began walking down the long table and marveled at all the beautiful baked goods.

"Wow, it's going to be hard to choose. This is better than a bakery."

"You bet. We've got some of the best cooks in the county in this church. We sell a cookbook too. It's down there on the end." As Charlotte walked down to look at it, Mrs. Donahue had an idea. "Would you do me a favor?"

"Sure."

"Pastor Gordon's in his office. Would you take him this pouch of money to put in his desk? I was going to take it, but I'd better stay here to man the table."

Charlotte looked around. There were only a couple of other people there, but she was glad to do a favor for this nice woman. She took the pouch and went down the hall to the pastor's office. Through the window, she could see him with a pen and paper and his Bible open. She knocked, and he looked up. He gave her a small smile and motioned her in. "Mrs. Donahue wanted me to bring you this." She held out the pouch of money.

"Thank you. I didn't know you were helping with the bake sale."

"I'm not. I just took a break from writing and stopped by."

"So, you're working on another book?"

"Yes. This one's set in the South Pacific."

"Nice." He nodded his head slowly. "Have you ever thought of writing a different kind of book?"

"What kind?"

"I don't know. One that's more useful for people. One that's not a romance."

Charlotte felt angry; angrier than his comments warranted. "What's wrong with a romance?"

"Don't you think it's kind of frivolous?"

"Not at all. The Bible's full of romance. Abraham and Sarah, Isaac and Rebekah, Jacob and Rachel, to name a few. Then there's the Song of Solomon."

"Yes, but..."

"But what?" she challenged a little more vehemently than she meant to. "If you think about it, romance is central to the whole message of Christ. The church is called the bride of Christ and His pursuit of us is the ultimate romance. We should be wildly in love with Him in response to his overtures toward us. He's the bridegroom we all need."

Pastor Gordon started at her, frozen and unable to say a word. He felt the same attraction to her that he thought he'd rid himself of forever. He really liked this woman. He was afraid to speak at all for fear he'd reveal his true feelings. So he just stared. After a moment of this, Charlotte began to giggle. "Have I struck you dumb? Or are you so annoyed with me that you don't even want to talk to me?"

Gordon managed a smile and simply answered, "I stand corrected. We'd both better get back to work." He looked back down at his notepad and she turned to leave. When she got to the door, she said, "Have I offended you?"

He shook his head, "Not at all. I'm impressed." But he put his head resolutely back down, so Charlotte left the room. There was something infuriating about that man.

Frank didn't call back until late into the evening. Since it was too late to go the movies that night, they decided to go to a matinee Sunday after church.

He picked her up right on schedule. Pastor Gordon noticed once again, but this time it was painful. He began to wish he'd never laid eyes on Charlotte Fyne.

She once again enjoyed Frank's company. They both liked the action film they'd seen and talked about the intricacies of the plot on their way home. They also worked out the details of the double date the next weekend. It felt secure to have plans for the future. When he walked her to the door, he leaned over to give her a quick kiss on the cheek. She felt awkward and decided not to invite him in.

Charlotte had just taken her shoes off and settled into a chair, when she heard a knock at the door. She opened it expecting to see Frank again, but instead a young girl stood in her doorway. She looked to be about ten, but Charlotte wasn't a good judge of age. "Yes?"

"Are you Charlotte Fyne?"

"Yes, I am."

"I thought so. You look just like your picture on your book covers."

"You've seen my books?"

"Yea, my mom buys them all and I read them when she's done with them."

"Oh." Charlotte wasn't sure what to do next. "How old are you?"

"I'm twelve, but I look young for my age." She shifted her weight to her other foot, looking uncomfortable. "Can I come in?"

Now Charlotte was confused. "I guess so. Did you want anything in particular?"

The girl walked right in and sat down on her sofa. "I want some advice."

"Advice?" Charlotte felt like she was in the twilight zone or something.

"Yea, advice about my love life."

That got Charlotte's attention. She sat down with a thud. "Aren't you a bit young to have a love life?"

"I told you I was twelve," she said looking indignant.

"Does your mother know you're here?"

"She's the one who told me to come." The girl looked like she'd about had it with this line of questioning.

"Okay, would you like a cookie or anything?"

"Sure!"

Charlotte went into the kitchen and came back with a plate of bake sale cookies and a couple of glasses of milk. "These're good," the girl proclaimed as she stuffed one into her mouth.

"I'm glad you like them. What's your name, anyway?"

"Misty."

"Well, Misty. What's the problem with your love life?"

"I ain't got one."

"I see." That's what Charlotte said, but she didn't see at all. "How can I help with that?"

"Tell me how to get one."

Charlotte sighed as she took in Misty's little girl demeanor. She hadn't developed much yet and looked like the kind of girl who would always have a baby face. She imagined that she had trouble keeping up with her classmates in the social arena.

"You'll have to help me. I'm rusty. How does a love life look to a twelve year old?"

"Huh?"

"What would you like to see happen?"

"I'd like the boys to like me. Everyone's got a boyfriend but me."

"I see." This seemed to be all Charlotte could get out as she silently prayed, "Help me, God. I have no idea what to say to this child."

"What would you do with this boyfriend?"

"Kiss and stuff."

Charlotte smiled, "Now do you see anyone kissing in my books?"

"Yea, they always do. Right when they ask them to marry them."

"Exactly. The characters in my books are all older. They're ready to make lifetime commitments. What you're seeing the other kids do at school is not what love is about at all. They're just seeing who will give them the most attention. They don't care about the person they like in the long run. That's why young love is so dangerous."

Misty screwed up her mouth until it touched her nose. "I was afraid you'd say that. That's what my mom says too."

Charlotte felt very relieved to hear that she and Misty's mom were on the same page. She'd been starting to wonder about her. "I think what you really want is to know that guys find you attractive. We all want to know that, even me."

"Yea, how do I know anyone ever will?"

"I guess you don't know for sure. So that's why we need to find our value in something besides whether or not a guy likes us."

"Like what?"

"Like the fact that God values us no matter what. That's the most important. Also we need to develop our abilities so we get satisfaction out of our accomplishments, as well as getting to know other people of all ages that we can be useful to." Charlotte took a bite of cookie. "In spite of my books, television, the movies, and all the talk at the junior high, there is more to life than romance."

Misty folded her legs under her and settled in more comfortably. "So you aren't married either?"

"No, I'm not."

"Does that ever make you sad?"

"Sometimes it makes me really sad, but then I have to concentrate on all the things I just told you and remember them myself. I have a great life. A man in it would be nice, but not necessary."

"Do you think I could bring some of my friends over once in a while and you could tell them this stuff too? Nobody my age seems to know it."

That caused Charlotte to chuckle. "Not too many people my age know it either." She took a sip of her milk which left a funny little mustache that made Misty laugh. "Sure, I'd like that. Just call before you come over, so that I'm prepared."

Unexpectedly Misty jumped up and hugged Charlotte. "Bye. I gotta go, but I'll be back. You're the greatest." Then she ran out the door as if she were in the Boston marathon.

Charlotte picked up the plates and glasses and carried them into the kitchen. "I guess I'd better listen to my own advice." She sat down at the kitchen table and spent a long time reading her Bible, ridding her mind of Frank and Gordon and even Misty's grade school heart throbs.

CHAPTER TWELVE

On Wednesday morning Mrs. Donahue called Charlotte to invite her over for lunch. "I just finished one of your novels."

"Which one?"

"*Love Dawns*."

"Did you like it?"

"I loved it. It's the most refreshing thing I've read in ages. That's why I want to have you over. I want to talk about it." Then she paused, "Is that all right? Do authors want to talk about their books? I mean, you're the first author I've ever known."

"I don't know about other authors, but I'd be glad to talk about it."

"Good, I'll see you about noon then."

"I'll bring some bake sale cake."

"That would be nice. It's Mrs. Snyder's cake isn't it?"

"I'm not sure."

"The one with caramel and chocolate on the top?"

"That's the one."

"Mmm. I can almost taste it now."

Charlotte got off the phone and sat back down at her computer. She liked Mrs. Donahue. She was the kind of person that made you feel like part of the family instantly. The morning flew by and when she next looked up it was eleven forty-five. She shut down her computer, pulled out the cake, and slipped on her shoes. After running a comb through her hair, she walked around the block.

"Welcome, Charlotte. Thanks for coming on such short notice."

"Thanks for asking."

She took the cake from her and almost hugged it. "Maybe we should skip lunch and just eat this."

"That's okay with me."

"But then all the beautiful cold cuts I set out would go to waste, and I'd never be able to scold Mort for not finishing his vegetables. Being a mother is such a grave responsibility." She shook her head and looked serious, but Charlotte saw the twinkle in her eye that showed she was teasing.

Mrs. Donahue had fresh flowers on the table which was set with her best china on a white tablecloth. “Wow, this is beautiful. I’ve never eaten cold cuts in such a lovely setting.”

“I love to make things look pretty. With four kids, everything was a mess for years. I’m enjoying doing the little extras I never had time for before.”

“How old are your other children?”

“All grown. The oldest is twenty-eight and the youngest twenty-three. As you can tell, Mort was an afterthought.”

“Yes. He’s a lot further behind.”

“When I found out I was pregnant with him, I almost collapsed, but he’s been a delight. I think I’ve enjoyed him more than all the others put together. Not that I love him more; just enjoy him.”

Charlotte nodded as they sat down at the table. For a few minutes they grew quiet as they made their sandwiches and took that first hungry bite. “So what did you want to talk about?”

“Oh, the young man in your story. I fell in love with him. You portrayed him so strong and sensitive. He reminded me of Pastor Gordon.”

Charlotte began choking and had to take a couple of drinks before she could speak. “Excuse me. I guess my food went down the wrong way.” After another drink she asked, “Why would you say that?”

Mrs. Donahue acted as if nothing had happened. “He’s the strong, quiet type. He seems all composed on the outside but is really a pushover on the inside.”

“That’s what you think Pastor Gordon is like?”

“Not think. I know. He’s almost like family to us. Everyone sees him as the confirmed bachelor who doesn’t need anyone, but I know differently.”

“How do you know that?”

“Little things he says and does. All the local women have given up on him but I don’t think they should have. They just have to be a little more persistent. Just like Mirabel was with Marcus in your story.”

“Well, you could have fooled me.”

Mrs. Donahue sighed, “I know. He’s fooled everyone including himself. If he’d just take that first step, I know he’d be over the hump. Maybe you’re the one to push him over the edge.”

“Me!” Charlotte looked at her as if she’d suggested that she actually kill Pastor Gordon. “Why me?”

“Because he likes you.”

"That's ridiculous. He can't stand me. He thinks all the romance novel stuff is foolish, and he doesn't like to be around me."

Mrs. Donahue looked like a wise sage as she narrowed her eyes and pursed her lips. "You make him nervous because he likes you."

"Are you sure about that?"

Mrs. Donahue put her sandwich down and rubbed her napkin over her mouth. "Oh, I guess I'm not sure. It's just a hunch. Besides, I think you'd be perfect for him."

"I see. Well, no disrespect intended, but I think you're dead wrong about this one. I've rarely felt such hostility from a man. He may need a woman, but it isn't me." As soon as Charlotte said this, she felt sad. She knew it was true, but startled herself by feeling bad about it. "Besides, I've been seeing Frank Rubin."

"Really," Mrs. Donahue looked surprise, "I hadn't heard about that. The Crispens Point grapevine must have a few breaks."

"It's not like we're serious or anything, but we are both enjoying each other's company right now."

"Well, that's nice. I'm sorry if I've interfered in your personal business. I didn't mean to. I was honest in the fact that I thought Marcus in your story reminded me of Gordon. I just thought you'd make a cute couple."

"No offense taken. Pastor Gordon's a great guy. I hope he finds someone."

"Oh he will eventually. At least if I have anything to do about it." She smiled like the Queen of Hearts in Alice in Wonderland right before she says, "Off with his head." Charlotte had no doubt that Mrs. Donahue would do her best to see Pastor Gordon married. As soon as the thought went through her mind, she felt sad again. The idea of him marrying someone made her feel awful. What was wrong with her?

After they'd both eaten all the cake they could without being ill, Charlotte walked slowly back home. Thoughts were circling her mind like vultures about to attack. "I thought I'd gotten over my initial attraction to Gordon McCrae, but maybe I haven't." Then the side of her that was more practical argued, "Well, I'd just better get over him. It's ridiculous to continue to moon over someone who could care less. Better the bird in the hand than two in the bush. I need to enjoy Frank and concentrate on him right now rather than pie in the sky that can never be. Besides, Frank's sweet. I really do like him."

She walked into her living room and laid down on the sofa. Suddenly she was so tired that all she could do was go to sleep.

When Friday came, Charlotte was still feeling blue but when Janice and Victor arrived at her door, she perked right up. A few minutes later Frank roared into the driveway in his little corvette. He bounced up to the door with another bouquet of flowers in his hands. Charlotte had just thrown out last week's the day before. She'd never been courted so lavishly before and she was enjoying it.

Janice introduced Victor to Frank and although both had been in high school at the same time, they couldn't really remember each other. But they seemed to get along well now and chatted like old friends. They had decided to go out for pizza and go bowling. So Charlotte, dressed casually, slipped into the back seat of Victor's van since four couldn't fit in Frank's car. Frank slid in after her and put his arm around her, pulling her close. It was the nearest they'd been physically, and Charlotte felt a little funny about it. Kind of like when in grade school, the boy you like chooses to sit next to you on the bus. Her breathing slowed and she was afraid to move. It made her mad that she felt so childish.

Victor and Janice talked and laughed, acting like an old married couple. They seemed completely at ease with each other. Despite all her reservations about Janice's pronouncements of being in love, she had to admit it looked to be true. Both of them appeared to be crazy about the other one, without being ridiculous about it. It made Charlotte feel jealous. Victor had struck her as sober and rather sad when she first met him but now he cracked jokes and laughed like a hyena. Janice looked at him with affection.

At one point in the evening when the men were buying cokes at the bowling alley, Charlotte asked Janice how she'd gotten along with Victor's daughter at the zoo. "Oh Charlotte, it was great. She clung to me like I was her long lost aunt. I'm absolutely in love with her, as much as I'm in love with her dad. This whole thing is too good to be true."

Charlotte smiled and didn't feel a bit like scolding Janice. She felt tremendously happy for her, and a little bit sad for herself.

When the guys came back, Frank handed Charlotte a coke. "So how good of a bowler are you?"

"Not very good. I haven't been in years."

"So are you saying that I should pick Victor as my partner instead of you?"

"Well!" She tried to act indignant. "That's not very loyal."

"Ah, I'm kidding. You're way prettier than Victor." He cuffed her chin lightly and her spirits rose. After that, things got better between them and by the end of the evening, she felt content.

The next Sunday at church, Charlotte felt a little bit of a jump in her heart when Pastor Gordon got up to speak. Mrs. Donahue's words echoed in her mind, making her mad that these futile thoughts were stirred up again.

When the service was over, she went through the line to congratulate Gordon on his good sermon. "Thank you, Pastor. Another excellent reminder." He gave her a polite smile as he shook her hand then quickly turned to the next person in line. "Nope," she thought, "I don't care how well Mrs. Donahue thinks she knows him, there's nothing there. So Charlotte, stop thinking about him right now."

These scoldings worked pretty well but she was annoyed when writing later that she kept picturing Pastor Gordon as the hero in her story. She purposely pasted Frank's image in her mind instead and resolutely disciplined his image into her character. It was fairly easy to do, because he fit the typical man in her stories. Handsome, caring and attentive, she willed herself to fall in love with him.

It had been a dreadfully hot day, so she closed everything up and turned on her air conditioner. A little while later, she heard a siren go off. She'd noticed that the wind had picked up because her windows were rattling as if someone was shaking them. So the siren worried her. Turning on the radio, she heard that a tornado was headed her way. She wasn't sure what to do since she didn't have a cellar to hide in. There were no rooms in her house without windows, so she hunched down in the hallway and waited. She'd been in a tornado once as a child and had been terrified of them ever since. All she had to do was close her eyes and the memory of the windows blowing in came back to her. It took her years to get over the terror she felt in any storm. While she sat their trembling, her phone rang. Grabbing the cordless, she took it back with her to the hallway.

"Charlotte, are you okay?"

"Oh Frank, I'm so glad you called. I'm really scared."

"Do you want me to come get you?"

"I don't think that would be wise. We'd better both stay inside."

"I've got a basement, at least. Where are you going to go?"

"I'm in the hallway. Tell you what, will you pray with me? My heart's beating awfully fast."

There was an awkward silence on the other end. "You mean like now, out loud?"

"Yes, it would be comforting."

Another moment of silence, then urgency in his voice: "Whoa, I hear rain coming down. I'd better go. I'll call when this is over."

Charlotte hung up the phone and a tear came to her eye. She felt so alone. She put her head down between her knees and trembled like a frightened bunny.

A few blocks away, Pastor Gordon made a few calls too. He was particularly worried about the shut-ins that he visited regularly. After making sure they had a place to take shelter, he prayed with each of them to calm their hearts. When he'd hung up, he thought of Charlotte. He wasn't sure what made him do it, but he threw on his rain coat and fought his way down the block to her house. Once there, he felt foolish. He knew he couldn't knock on her door, but he was worried about her, so he placed a hand on the outside of her house and prayed that God would keep her safe. He knelt down in the bushes and stayed there until the storm had passed.

Inside her house, Charlotte felt a peace come over her. The frustration she'd felt a moment earlier lifted. She wondered if perhaps Frank had prayed for her after all, or if God knew she needed His presence and sent His Holy Spirit to comfort her. Either way, she relaxed and drifted into the knowledge of His love.

The tornado touched down on the edge of town, tearing into an apartment building, collapsing one of the residences. Fortunately, the occupants had evacuated, so no one was hurt. True to his word, Frank not only called, but jumped in his car to see if Charlotte was safe. On his way there, he passed a figure that was drenched walking away from Charlotte's neighborhood. He wondered who would have been foolish enough to be out in this storm.

Running up to her door, he banged on it with his fist. She opened it timidly, but when she saw Frank all the tension she'd been feeling drained out of her. She fell into his arms sobbing, and he comforted her like a child. Although startled at her reaction, he enjoyed the feel of her body close to his and her obvious need of his presence. He reluctantly let her go when she finally pulled away. He wanted to kiss her more than he'd ever wanted anything. He'd been so patient, and it had been too long since he'd been with a woman, but he instinctively knew this wasn't the time. He'd wait a bit longer. She'd eventually be ready.

From across the street Mrs. Bartholomew saw everything. She saw Pastor Gordon get up out of the bushes and walk away when the storm passed. She saw Frank arrive and Charlotte's obvious relief as she clung to him. Hugging Custer, who had been clinging to her ever since the storm began, she said, "Something's very strange over there. What are we going to do about it, old boy?"

CHAPTER THIRTEEN

The next day Misty showed up on Charlotte's doorstep with two of her friends. "Hi. You said I could bring some people over, so here we are." She looked as cheerful as if she'd brought Charlotte a Christmas present.

"I think I told you to call first," Charlotte said gently without reproof in her voice.

"Oh yea, I forgot." She scratched her head and then asked, "Do you want me to go home and call you?" This was a girl who lived by the rules when she remembered them.

Charlotte laughed, "No, just try to remember next time. Come on in."

The other two girls hid behind Misty until they walked into the house, then they began to act more comfortable. They bounced on the sofa, looking like they planned to settle in for the winter. When everyone was seated, they all looked awkwardly at each other. Finally Charlotte broke the silence, "What exactly can I do for you girls?"

The two new girls looked at Misty. Misty looked back at them and shrugged her shoulders. Finally one of the girls said, "We want you to tell us about having boyfriends and stuff like that."

Charlotte's face was a complete blank but her mind was racing. "What in the world am I going to tell these girls? This is ridiculous." But out loud she said, "Why don't we start with names. You can call me Charlotte."

"We know that," said the taller of the two girls. "Misty gives us your books to read."

"Okay, so why don't you tell me who you are."

The same girl spoke again. She seemed to be the leader. "I'm Nanette, and this is Virginia." She pointed to the pale blond who looked as if she'd rather stay invisible.

"Good. Well, I was just working on another book."

"What's this one about?"

"It's about a woman who meets a man in the South Pacific but thinks he doesn't care for her, so they almost don't get together when she returns to the United States."

"Ooh, that sounds good. Tell us more."

So Charlotte started telling them the story in detail. After about twenty minutes had gone by, she pulled out the last of her bake sale items, and they munched on goodies as she finished the tale. It took a while because of all the questions they asked her about her character's love life. Every once in a while, she'd have to remind them that the people in her stories were imaginary, since they began to ask what happened after the story ended. They seemed disappointed about the reminder.

"Now you girls know more than anyone. You won't have to read the book."

"I'll read it anyway," said Nanette. "I get more of the details that way. Besides you didn't tell us exactly how it ends. You made us guess. So we'll have to read it to see which one of us was right."

Charlotte smiled. She liked these girls. Her life had revolved around adults for so long that she'd forgotten how refreshing children could be.

"Can we come back next week, so you can tell us some more?"

"Sure, just remember to call." She emphasized the word, call.

They all nodded their heads and took off through the door. Summer gets long for twelve year olds.

A week later, when she responded to a knock on her door, five girls stood there looking at her eagerly. When she reminded them about the fact that they were supposed to call, they looked stricken. "Oh never mind, come on in. But the problem is that I don't have anything prepared to eat."

"That's okay," said Misty. "I'll run home and get some microwave popcorn. Is it okay if I use your microwave?"

"That would be fine. I think I have some lemonade I can mix up. Will that do with popcorn?" All five heads nodded, so she took that as a yes.

"Don't say anything important until I get back," yelled Misty as she took off down the block.

By the time Misty returned, Charlotte had them organized into sections so that they could write their own romance. They set up the characters and she gave each girl an assignment. After each person contributed and the final story came together, it was hilarious. Even Charlotte laughed so hard that her sides hurt.

As they started to leave, one of the newest girls said to Charlotte, "You are so beautiful. I hope I get prettier."

Charlotte studied her. The girl was certainly at an awkward stage in life. With both glasses and braces and blemishes threatening to take over, she looked to be the ugly duckling. Charlotte remembered those days well enough. "Do you know I looked quite a bit like you when I was your age? Nobody noticed me. But the good thing about that was I learned to develop other things, like my writing. Concentrating on who I was rather than what I looked like was the best thing for me. It can also make us pay attention to God. Otherwise, we skip along our merry way without giving Him a thought. Maybe He's whispering to you right now."

The girl's eyes got bigger and she asked, "How will I know if He's talking to me?"

"You'll understand more about Him. He says, after all, that if we seek Him with all our hearts, we'll find Him. It's the best adventure we can undertake in life."

"Wow, you ought to be a preacher or something."

"Oh no. I do better writing my thoughts rather than saying them aloud. I'll stick to that." Charlotte smiled, "Plus, no one can talk back to me in my books!"

Something about the girls leaving made Charlotte reflect. So far she'd been concentrating on her own well-being and comfort since she'd moved to Crispens Point. Their presence made her think about what she wanted to give back to the community. She pulled out her church bulletin and browsed through it, looking for opportunities to serve. Her interest peaked when she read about the youth group activities. Her experience with the girls gave her confidence that she had something to offer this age group. She decided to call Mrs. Donahue. "Hello, this is Charlotte. How are you today?"

“I’m doing fine. What’s up?”

“I was wondering if you could use some help with youth group. I’ve never done anything like that, but I’d like to try.”

“How did you know?”

“Know what?”

“That we needed help? I just called the secretary, and we put an announcement in the bulletin for this Sunday. Our youth group is growing so rapidly that we need more adults.”

“That’s great. What do you want me to do?”

“Our planning meeting is tomorrow night at my house. Seven o’clock. Just show up and we’ll get to work.”

“Sounds good. I’ll see you then.”

Charlotte hung up the phone with a feeling of contentment. Maybe God allowed her to be single so that she’d have time for stuff like this. It made her glad for the first time that John had left her. She realized that it had been a long time since she’d thought of him. It was a relief to realize that no matter what John’s behavior had been, that she was exactly where God wanted her. She was starting to fall in love with Crispens Point.

Tuesday flew by as Charlotte concentrated on her work. Around six o'clock she popped a microwave meal in and polished it off, as if she'd been starved as a child. After washing up the few dishes, she grabbed a notebook and set off around the block. She thought of the countless times she'd raced for the train in the city and delighted in how simple her life had become.

Mrs. Donahue had iced tea and lemonade for everyone as they gathered around her table. "Charlotte, this is Bill and Sara Michaels. They help with youth group too."

"Nice to meet you." Charlotte extended her hand to shake with both of them.

"The only one left is Pastor. He should be here any minute."

"He helps with youth group too?" Charlotte asked, trying not to reveal how her heart raced.

"Yes, he does all the devotionals. He's also speaking at the upcoming retreat."

"Oh, when is the retreat?"

"Next weekend. I'm sorry, Charlotte. I should have told you about it when you volunteered. Don't feel like you have to come along."

"I'd be glad to come. I don't have anything going this weekend. How many kids are going?"

Mr. Donahue piped up, "Too many!"

Mrs. Donahue punched him in the arm. "One is too many for Morton, but he's a good sport to go along anyway. Actually, we have the largest group ever; about thirty-five are going."

"Wow, that is a bunch. I can see why you needed more help."

At that moment, the door slammed in the living room, "I just let myself in," Pastor Gordon's baritone voice boomed through the house.

"We're in the kitchen. Come on in."

Gordon stepped through the door with a broad smile on his face. When he saw Charlotte, his face fell as if he'd just seen the Grim Reaper. "Hello," he said in a distracted way. "Am I at the right meeting?"

"Of course you are. What a silly question."

Mr. Donahue came to his rescue, "Charlotte volunteered to help out with youth group. Isn't that nice, Pastor?" He looked at Gordon with concern.

"Very nice," he said smoothly, recovering at least in part, but he sat as far away from her as possible.

They got down to business, and the evening trickled away just as sand in an hour glass drifts on. Charlotte said little but listened attentively, hoping she'd be prepared for this undertaking. She'd liked being with the junior high girls, but these were high school kids and she didn't know if she'd be as good with that age group, but she was willing to try. She'd learned years ago that her faith grew the quickest when she tried things that made her feel insecure. Somehow doing the difficult made her depend on God more and get to know Him better. So, she looked on this as an adventure.

The rest of the week was fairly uneventful. When she told Janice what she was doing, Janice told her she was crazy, but said it affectionately so Charlotte wasn't offended. She even suggested that Janice come along, but Janice said, "No way. Besides, I'd have to leave Victor for the weekend. I'd miss him too much." She said this so cheerfully that it made Charlotte feel like pinching her, just to make her more sober. It also dawned on her that she hadn't even thought of telling Frank she was leaving, so she gave him a call when she hung up with Janice.

"I just wanted you to know that I'll be gone this weekend."

"You're taking me away for a romantic getaway." Frank said this in his boyish manner which made him so irresistible.

"No, I'm going away with thirty-five high school kids."

"Oh yuck. I think I'd rather be ill with the flu."

Charlotte laughed, and their conversation ended a few minutes later with Frank telling her he'd miss her.

On Friday afternoon Charlotte packed enough for two days and two nights and drove her vehicle for the first time to church since she'd need to take a car load of kids with her. Several of the kids looked at her shyly, obviously wondering what she was doing there. She sought out Mrs. Donahue to get her marching instructions. "Who goes with me?"

"I think I'll put Louisa, Marcie, and JoAnn in your car. Don't worry, they're the easy ones. The most rambunctious boys go with Morton and me, and the least rambunctious go in the church van with Pastor. It would be too much for him otherwise. The Michaels are driving their van with everyone else."

Charlotte glanced over at Pastor as he good naturedly patted a teenager on the back. He seemed comfortable with all ages. She followed Mrs. Donahue's pointing finger to a cluster of girls in front of the church doors. After introducing herself, she announced who was going with her. Three girls who looked to be sixteen or seventeen followed her to her car. "I hope you don't mind going with the new person," Charlotte said, hoping to break the ice.

One of them smiled showing a mouth full of perfect teeth that probably cost her parents a bundle. "You're the romance writer, aren't you?"

"I am, but I'm a lot more besides. I hope you'll be able to get to know another side of me this weekend."

"But we want to know about the romance side," added Louisa, the plainest of the three but the liveliest. "Only JoAnn is dating someone." She stuck out her tongue at the only girl who hadn't spoken yet. JoAnn pushed her sideways in response, looking like a mother dog who was annoyed with her pup.

"Well, I probably won't be much help. I've been single for a long time. That's probably why I began making my relationships up in stories."

This brought a laugh from all of them. Charlotte thought about how quickly the ice was broken with young people. They haven't built up all the suspicions and wariness that adults immediately display. After buckling seat belts and waiting for the lead car, they took off for Camp Tohika.

Charlotte enjoyed the ride. They passed rolling fields of corn, bright red barns in need of repair, and pastures full of horses and cattle. The girls laughed and sang, making Charlotte kind of crazy by the end, but the overall cheerfulness of the girls made her happy. They pulled into the camp just an hour later.

The camp was set in a vast pine woods with a small lake in the middle. The lodge where they would stay was made of rough-hewn cedar logs, both inside and out. The males would stay on one side of the lodge and the females on the other. A large meeting room with a fireplace and open beams separated the two wings. Charlotte admired the large Native American blankets that covered the walls for decoration. Best of all was the view that overlooked the lake.

She took her bedding into the bunk house and chose a bottom bunk on the far corner before they all were taken. It was a fruitless worry since all the girls fought over the top bunks. She made up her bed then sat on it as it sank down at least a foot. Oh well, nothing was perfect.

The first item on the agenda was dinner so the gang walked in a large group to the dining hall. As soon as Pastor Gordon prayed, the hungry teens descended on the buffet line like hungry wolves. He hung back with the other adults and commented, "Maybe we should make a rule that adults go first so that there will be some left."

Mr. Donahue chuckled. "That sounds good to me. If I don't get fed this weekend, I'll get real grumpy. Won't I, Sweetie Pie?" And he pinched Mrs. Donahue right on the bottom. She smacked his hand and acted annoyed, but you could see the delight on her face in spite of her outward actions.

At long last, the line dwindled and the adults found plenty to eat. After settling at a table together, they discussed the evening's plans. Pastor had a devotional planned followed by several games that the Michaels would direct. Charlotte was glad that she was there mostly for crowd control.

The evening went smoothly and Charlotte stayed up into the wee hours visiting with the girls who had, like her, drifted to the room early to retire. As it turned out, they enjoyed conversing so much that they were still awake when curfew was called at midnight. They all declared that they were much too excited to go to sleep, so whispers continued long after the lights went out. Mrs. Donahue finally announced that enough was enough, and snores were heard throughout the room a few minutes later.

Morning dawned much too soon but the promise of pancakes got most of the kids out of bed on time, especially the boys. After breakfast, lots of singing followed with Bill playing the guitar, and Pastor gave another devotional. Then all the students were divided into small groups. Since Charlotte was new, she was given the fewest girls so she had only five. Pastor gave her some questions to ask them, which she didn't have time to read beforehand. In spite of that, they went smoothly until Charlotte got to the fifth question. "How do you think Jesus wants us to act around the opposite sex?" Then all hell broke loose. Literally.

"My dad says girls should wear clothes that cover their whole body. He wants me to go around wearing turtlenecks and long pants, even in the summer. I often change clothes as soon as I've left the house."

"We all know that, JoAnn. You've been doing that since sixth grade. Everyone knows that except your dad."

"Yea, what about my mom?" added another girl. "She won't let me date until I'm eighteen. How fair is that? I can't even go to a school dance until I'm a senior. By then all the boys will have given up on me. I'll be an old maid."

"I'd hardly call eighteen an old maid," Charlotte began, but got cut off right away by Marcie. "I think all our parents are totally out of touch with what it's like to be a teenager. They should have to go back for a day and see what it's like. One afternoon at my school and they'd be screaming for mercy."

"I'm dying to make out with a guy. What's it like, JoAnn?" Obviously JoAnn was the experienced one in the group. But Charlotte felt the discussion was as out of control as a runaway skateboard. "Enough, girls. We've gotten way off the track. The question is..."

"I'm going to move in with my boyfriend as soon as I'm eighteen," JoAnn declared.

"Good grief," thought Charlotte. And I've got the good girls?

"How cool!" chorused all but Louisa. She seemed to be very sober.

"It's not cool!" yelled Charlotte and the group suddenly looked at her as if they'd forgotten she was there.

"Oh come on, you're a romance writer. You're used to this kind of stuff." JoAnn looked disgusted.

So that's what's going on, thought Charlotte. "Contrary to what you may think romance can have moral guidelines. For heaven's sakes, God invented romance in the first place."

The girls stared at her shocked. Such a thought had never occurred to them. Louisa looked like she'd been given a brand new shiny penny. "You mean God approves of romance?"

"Of course, He does. It's just that He's given us parameters so that we don't hurt ourselves and others."

"Will you teach us?"

"Teach you what?"

"A Bible study on what God has to say about romantic relationships." Louisa was in charge now, and the others looked at her with interest.

This worried Charlotte a little. For all her defense of romance, she didn't have a lot of concrete ideas to back it up, but something about Louisa's face made her want to find out. "I guess so. I'd have to give it some thought."

"Can we invite our friends?" asked Marcie. Louisa's attitude had obviously infected her. In fact, all the girls seemed to have a renewed interest, except for JoAnn. She looked skeptical.

"Sure. Just give me some time to think about it."

This seemed to satisfy the girls and Charlotte was able to finish the questions. She imagined that Pastor Gordon had no idea the fervor his simple outline would cause.

The afternoon was taken with swimming, which involved the girls being regularly thrown in the water by the boys. At dinner the staff once again convened. "How did your discussion questions go?" Pastor asked. Various comments were made, and Charlotte just nodded her head when Sara looked at her. "Louisa told me you were going to do a Bible study with them about romance."

Charlotte turned red, but answered, "Yes, question number five was kind of like a bomb for our group. Did anyone else have trouble with that one?"

They all shook their heads which made Charlotte turn even redder. "Well, my girls had a lot of misconceptions and a lot of resentment toward their parents."

"The girls I gave you?" Mrs. Donahue looked astonished. "Why I'd say they are the least rebellious girls in town."

Charlotte shrugged her shoulders. "I don't know, but they sure assaulted me with questions."

"Maybe it was the nature that you posed the question."

Charlotte cringed when she heard Gordon's voice, but something about his accusation made her angry, "That may well be, but I got some honest answers and I'm not content to let the girls continue on in the ideas they've developed."

Pastor nodded, "I'd like to see that study when you put it together." She frowned. "Not that I don't trust you or anything." He said this with a straight face, but she felt sure there was some sarcasm hidden there. Nevertheless she agreed. The rest of the group moved on to other topics, but Charlotte ate in silence. Pastor Gordon could make her furious.

Charlotte was relieved that Saturday night's discussion group went well. Fortunately there weren't any questions about relationships. The girls settled down to sleep a little easier that night and Sunday morning's worship time was delightful, with kids sharing how the weekend had changed their lives.

Arriving back in Crispens Point, kids and adults alike looked haggard but happy. Charlotte was glad she'd volunteered for this, but she went home relieved she'd not need to sit under Pastor Gordon's disapproval any more.

CHAPTER FOURTEEN

Charlotte had just gotten back and put her feet up when her phone rang. Hoping it was Frank, she answered quickly.

"Hello little girl."

"Oh, hi Mom. How was your weekend?"

"Not very good." Her mother sounded so weary that Charlotte could almost feel the heaviness through the phone. "I hate to just drop this on you, but I had a bad visit to the doctor yesterday."

Charlotte's heart raced, "What do you mean?"

"I didn't tell you before, because I didn't want to alarm you, but I found a lump on my breast." As soon as Charlotte heard those words, she wished she could hang up the phone and pretend she'd never heard from her mom. "They did a biopsy last week and found cancer."

"Oh no, Mom. Are they sure?"

"I'm afraid they are."

"Well, you can beat this. Lots of women have breast cancer." Her mom suddenly gave a sob which made Charlotte feel like someone had reached in and squeezed her heart. "What are they going to do?"

"I'm afraid I ignored this for too long. The cancer is everywhere. In my lymph nodes and even in my brain. They're going to do chemotherapy and radiation but I don't know..."

"No, Mom..." Charlotte felt the tears coming although they were unwanted. She hoped to be strong for her mother.

"Don't cry, honey. We'll just take one day at a time. I won't go home a day before Jesus wants me."

"It was bad enough losing Dad..." Charlotte's voice sounded like someone had run her voice box over sand paper. Her mother was silent. "You're all I have left."

"I know. I'm praying God will give you a husband before I go. So I guess you'd better put the pressure on Frank." She forced her tone to be cheerful but Charlotte knew it was an act.

Charlotte laughed which came out as a kind of snort. "No. I've got plenty of time. You'll be around for thirty more years at least."

"That would be nice." Her mother's melancholy spirit showed its true colors in this simple statement which made Charlotte sadder than anything else she'd said. "I'd better go now. I'll call when I know more."

"I love you, Mom."

"I love you, too, darling."

Charlotte clung to the phone a minute longer before she hung up as if doing this act would cause her mom to stay longer. When she finally put it down, she cried in earnest. About fifteen minutes later the phone rang again. She thought irrationally that her mom was calling back to let her know they'd found it to be a mistake, so she snatched it up and said, "Yes."

"Well hello, beautiful. I didn't know you'd be so eager to talk to me. A little time in the woods with all those teenagers makes me look pretty good, huh?" Frank's cheerful voice, which ordinarily made Charlotte feel good, now grated on her nerves.

"I'm sorry, Frank, I can't talk right now. I've just had really bad news."

"Are you okay?" His voice held alarm.

"Not really."

"I'll come right over."

"No!" Charlotte jumped at the power of her own voice. Frank did too. "I just need some time to process this, that's all. I'll call you tomorrow."

"I don't like this. Just blurt it out."

"My mom has cancer."

"Oh." His boyish manner came through more than ever. He didn't have any idea what to say so he just sat there silent. All that came to his mind was that he hoped she had a good insurance policy, which he knew wouldn't be good to say right now. Finally he said, "That is bad news. I'll wait for your call tomorrow," and he hung up the phone.

Charlotte put the phone down quickly this time. She'd never felt so alone.

When the phone rang again a little while later, she thought of not answering at all, but the thought that it might be her mom caused her to lift it to her ear one more time.

Charlotte?" She was startled to hear Pastor Gordon's voice.

"Yes."

"I'm sorry to bother you, but one of the girls in your car lost her purse. Did you happen to see it?"

"No, but I'll go look."

"That would be great. Do you want me to hold?"

"Sure."

Charlotte ran out to the garage. In the back seat a hand bag sat unclaimed. She pulled it out and went back to the phone. "Yes, I've got it."

"Great. Would you mind if I ran over to get it? She's kind of distressed."

"Okay." Charlotte felt like it wasn't okay at all. She had no desire to see Pastor Gordon, but she didn't see what she could do about it.

Hanging up the phone, she dried her tears. Looking in the mirror, she thought she looked awful. Her eyes were puffy, her nose red and she was even a bit dusty from camp. But none of that mattered. She certainly could care less what Pastor Gordon thought.

He knocked on her door a few minutes later, and she opened the door and handed him the purse without really looking at him. But he looked at her, perhaps more intently than he'd ever looked at her before. She looked terrible. "Are you all right?"

Charlotte just hung her head and nodded without convincing him in the least. "You don't look well. Can I do anything for you?"

"No, no one can do anything for me."

"Charlotte..." Something about the tender way he said her name made her look up.

"Yes?"

"Can I pray for you?"

At these words the tears began streaming down her cheeks again. She couldn't speak, so she just nodded. Standing in her doorway since she hadn't invited him in, Pastor Gordon prayed for her. "Dear Heavenly Father. You know what's making Charlotte so sad right now. I pray that You would lift her heart and help her to know that You are sufficient even for this difficult thing she is facing now. Wrap her in Your loving arms and fill her with Your presence. We pray in Jesus' name. Amen." Pastor Gordon looked at her one more time and turned away. He thought he needed to leave quickly before he took her in his arms and never let her go.

After he left, Charlotte felt more alone than ever. She sat on the sofa, staring out into the room, arguing with God about the unfairness of it all. Finally she took a warm bath and fell asleep as soon as her head hit the pillow.

The next morning she couldn't face working on her book, so she decided to spend it reading and praying, which was the advantage of being an author and determining her own schedule. When she could no longer sit still, she went for a long walk to clear her head. By the end of the day, she was somewhat renewed in her spirit, at least enough to get perspective on her week. She called her mom and offered to come and stay with her, but her mom resolutely refused. She was going to go to work as long as possible and carry on her life as usual. Charlotte had to admire her for that.

She eventually decided that she couldn't put off calling Frank anymore, although she didn't fell like it. Making herself push the buttons of his number, she was relieved when only the answering machine clicked on. Setting the phone back on its cradle, she decided against leaving a message.

A few minutes later the phone rang. She picked it up out of habit, dreading whoever it might be. She was surprised when she heard Louisa's voice, "Hi, Charlotte. I was wondering when we could start that Bible study. I told some more girls about it, and they want to come too."

Instead of being a burden, this gave Charlotte new energy. "I tell you what. Let's plan on next Monday night. Will that work?"

"Yea, that's great. Thanks!" And the conversation was over.

Charlotte immediately dialed her mother again. "Mom, I need your help."

"I'm not painting anything!" she said with laughter in her voice.

"No, I need to put together a Bible study on what God has to say about relationships for a group of high school girls. How about if I come over for the rest of the week? I'll write while you're at work, and in the evenings we can work on this study."

Her mom was silent for a minute and Charlotte was afraid she was going to refuse. To her relief, she said, "I'd like that."

"Great. I'll be there at about dinner time tomorrow. We'll go out to eat."

"Thanks, little girl. That's perfect." And she knew her mom meant it. She understood her mother well enough to realize that the reason she hadn't wanted Charlotte to come was that she didn't want them moping around in the evenings. With something specific to do, the dynamic of the week changed. "Thanks, God. You're timing is perfect."

She went to bed that evening feeling one hundred times better than the night before. It felt like being able to fly after crawling a long ways. After awaking Tuesday morning, she called Janice before work to tell her where she'd be and left a message on Frank's machine with the same information. It bothered her that she was once again relieved that he wasn't home. He was just too cheerful for times like these.

After doing laundry and paying her bills, she packed and put her suitcase in her car. She thought of Misty and her gang. They'd probably be by sometime this week and wonder what happened to her, but it couldn't be helped. Getting in the car, she almost felt lighthearted as she roared down the country roads toward the interstate. In just a couple of hours, she'd be there.

Pulling up to the little ranch style house that her father had built, she let herself in with the key she'd had since grade school. She'd often suggested that her mom move to a condo so she wouldn't have to worry about maintenance and the yard, but her mother wouldn't think of it. "No other place is going to have a pantry like this one that your dad made with shelves just right to fit my containers. And think of the built-in bookcases in my bedroom. Where would I put all my books? And the flower garden that Dad hauled in enough dirt to fill a sink hole in Florida. No, this is the place for me."

And now as Charlotte walked up to it, she felt relieved that her mom hadn't listened to her. It was awfully nice to be someplace familiar. And she knew her mom would get strength from this place to battle this cancer. She went around back to look at her Mom's flowers. They were perfect as usual. Charlotte leaned over to smell a rose that was as big as a saucer and as red as Marilyn Monroe's lips. She breathed in the sweet scent as if it were life giving oxygen.

She'd just gone inside when her mom returned. "How fun to come home and find you here; I thought maybe I'd beat you this afternoon."

"Not a chance." They hugged each other more intensely than usual and Charlotte noticed her mom had trouble letting go.

"Where do you want to eat?"

"Luigi's, of course. I've been hungry for it all day. It's a little early though."

"Oh well, let's beat the crowd. If I know you, you probably skipped lunch anyway."

Charlotte grinned, "I'm starving now that you've reminded me."

A few hours later they were back at home with commentaries, concordances, and several different translations spread around them. "I'm so glad you're doing this, Charlotte. Girls sure need to get this straight."

"You're telling me. I know that all too well." A confidential smile passed between Charlotte and her mom with just a hint of sadness.

After diligently working, they had the first lesson figured out. Charlotte felt quite pleased with it and her mom seemed just as satisfied. "This is fun. I haven't prepared a

Bible study in years. Maybe I should volunteer to teach Sunday school again."

"You're the best, Mom. You should. Those kids would love you. How could they not?"

"I guess I'd better wait and see how I feel after my first radiation treatment tomorrow night. I guess I'm going to lose my hair." Her mom looked sober.

"Let's go wig shopping when you get home from work tomorrow. It'll be fun."

She smiled slightly. "I've always wondered what I'd look like as a blond."

"This could be a blast. Why don't we pick out several wigs? You could have a different style and color every day."

"I like that idea." Her mom perked up now. "I always wanted to be kind of a splashy old lady. Maybe this is my chance."

"It's the perfect opportunity."

Charlotte and her mom had a great time. She tried on long, short and medium wigs that came in auburn, platinum blond, and raven black. She even put on an afro that set them both giggling until they could hardly stand up. They finally decided on a highlighted brown, a red-tinted brown and a brown that almost matched her own color for the days she wanted to be conventional. She felt quite happy with her choices, kind of like a little school girl who gets red and silver shoes as well as basic black. Charlotte stared at her as they walked out to the car and felt again that she was amazing.

The week ended on a happy note with all of the lessons finished. Saturday, she had another radiation treatment, which wore her out more this time. Charlotte rented a couple of movies and popped a giant bowl of popcorn. Fortunately it was raining, so the weather cooperated with their plans. She knew her mother would never sit inside on a nice day. On Sunday, they went to church together and Charlotte packed to go home. "Are you sure you don't want me to stay?"

"Nope, our mission's done. You have youth group tonight and a Bible study to lead Monday night. I have my Bunko group and the potluck at church Wednesday. Sorry, I'm too busy to fit you in." She said this with a smile, lifting her chin in a superior way. Charlotte hugged her and refused to cry, knowing that was the last thing her mom wanted. She thanked God again that when He chose a family for her to be in that He gave her this one. They'd prayed for a baby and when the adoption agency called them about Charlotte, it was no mistake.

She drove home feeling content and looking forward to youth group. She arrived at her house just in time for a quick bite to eat before heading over to the church. The girls from the retreat bounded up to her as if she were their long lost friend. When Pastor Gordon saw her his blood pressure raced, but he simply said, "Janice told us about your mom. We prayed for her as a group on Wednesday night."

"Thank you. That means a lot."

"You look like you're feeling better."

"I am." Then she braced herself for the next part. "By the way, here's the Bible study I'm doing with the girls. We're starting tomorrow night. I'm sorry for the short notice, but I just got back from my mom's."

"I'm sure it's fine, but I'd like to see it anyway. Go ahead with it. I think it's just what the girls need." She watched him walk up to the front of the room to open the meeting, wondering what the true Gordon McCrae thought about her. Maybe we've reached a truce. It was awfully nice of him to pray for me.

After a devotional, the group played games which Charlotte would have been glad to skip. It looked like most of the adults felt that way except for Mrs. Donahue. She was having the time of her life.

Charlotte woke up Monday morning filled with expectancy. She'd just filled her mug with coffee, when there was a knock at her door. "Hello. I know it's early but I've been worried about you." Mrs. Bartholomew stood there holding Custer. He looked lazily up at Charlotte through slitted eyes as if appraising whether or not she might have some fresh fish in the house.

"Oh, come in. Would you like a cup of coffee?"

"Yes, I would." As soon as she set Custer down, he dashed through the door, running to the kitchen to see what Charlotte had there. "Oh, I'm sorry. I'll put him out."

"That's okay. I like cats. He's welcome to stay."

Mrs. Bartholomew looked at Custer and pointed a finger at him. "Now listen, mister, you'd better behave. This isn't your house, you know." In answer he swished his tail, put his ears back and took a giant leap to the counter. "Why you rascal," she yelled, and she turned on the faucet, wetted her fingers and flicked water in his face. He jumped down and went to the corner to sulk. Mrs. Bartholomew shook her head, "I can't take him anywhere."

Charlotte managed to avoid giggling during this display while she poured coffee. Sitting down to the table, she said, "I'm sorry I didn't tell you I was leaving. I left in such a hurry. My mom just found out she has cancer, so I spent the week with her."

Mrs. Bartholomew's hand flew over her mouth, "Oh, stupid me. To think of all the unkind things that went through my mind. I was sure you'd run off with that Rubin boy."

Charlotte blushed, grabbed Mrs. Bartholomew's hand and said emphatically, "You don't ever have to worry about that happening. I'm very old-fashioned and won't run off with anyone until I've got a wedding dress on."

"Well, I'm glad to hear it." She nodded her head once looking like a judge. "And I'm sorry about your mother. I like her."

Charlotte knew this was a compliment rarely bestowed. They both sipped their coffee, and Charlotte decided that she'd best tell her as much as possible about everything so that she wouldn't jump to conclusions. "I'm helping with the youth group at church now, so every Monday a group of girls will be coming over."

"I know. I've seen them over here, although not always on a Monday."

"Oh, that's Misty and her friends; a different group. I never know when they're going to pop in."

"They came by last Wednesday, but left when no one answered the doorbell."

Charlotte nodded. Truly nothing would ever be a secret from Mrs. Bartholomew if she could help it.

As soon as Charlotte saw both her guests to the door, (it took some time to catch Custer) she thought of her answering machine. She'd been so busy that she hadn't checked it. There were about seven messages. The third one was from Frank, "I miss you, Charlotte. When are you going to call me?" He whined a bit, sounding like a little boy who's been denied his daily ice cream.

"Oh, Frank. How could I have neglected to call you?" She dialed the number and heard a sleepy voice, "Rubin Insurance, can I help you?"

"I don't know. Have you got any policies that will guarantee I live happily ever after?"

"Charlotte!" Frank sounded wide awake now. "When'd you get back?"

"Last night."

"I missed you."

"Thanks. It's nice to be home, but I worry about my mom."

"Oh yea," he said as if he'd forgotten all about her mom. "She okay?"

"She's doing amazingly well for all she's going through."

"Good for her." He paused a moment then asked, "So, let's go out to eat tonight. I'll pick you up about seven."

"I can't Frank. I have a group of high school girls coming to my house tonight."

"Well, cancel it."

"What?"

"Cancel it. I miss you. I want to be with you." He sounded annoyed.

She laughed as if he were joking, "Oh sure, Your Majesty. I'd hate to ruin your plans."

Then he knew she thought he was kidding and played along, "That's okay, Princess. If you're too busy for the white knight to rescue you..."

"How about tomorrow night?"

"I don't know. I've got a meeting." He didn't, but he liked feeling that he had important things to do without her.

"Thursday night, then."

"What happened to Wednesday?"

"I've got Bible study, remember?"

"Oh yea. You sure spend a lot of time at church."

"I guess I do," Charlotte laughed.

After she hung up the phone, Frank threw his pillow so hard against the wall that feathers flew out of it. He was tired of waiting for Charlotte. He needed her to want him as much as he wanted her. He wondered what he could do about that.

A little while later the phone rang. "Charlotte?"

"Yes?"

"This is Pastor Gordon. I just finished looking over your study. This looks great! I've never seen anything quite like it."

"Thank you."

"I'll be praying for your group tonight."

"I'd appreciate it, Pastor."

He hung up the phone smiling. He wished she wouldn't call him Pastor, though. She was one person he really wished would call him Gordon.

At precisely seven, Charlotte opened the door on the first knock. Louisa and Marcie stood there with two other girls Charlotte didn't know. "I think more are coming." Louisa walked in with the other three following her. A few minutes later two more girls came. Charlotte gave them all something to eat and drink, then they settled in on all the available chairs, with a few on the floor. She'd just started the study when a loud rap sounded at the door and JoAnn walked in. Charlotte was very glad to see her. She slunk in and slouched against the sofa as if she owned the place, "I'm giving this one night." She held up her pointer finger to indicate the number one and then pointed at Charlotte. "You have one chance, Lady."

Charlotte stared at her wide-eyed and looked around the room at the rest of the girls. They all looked back at her to see what she would do. "Thanks for giving it a chance, JoAnn. I'm glad you could come." In response, she closed her eyes halfway looking extremely bored. Charlotte looked away from her and continued. "We're going to start in the first chapter of Genesis and find out how God created women in the first place. If He made us, He must know better than any of us what He wants us to do. So let's start there."

The girls looked mesmerized as Charlotte wove the creation story and shared some things she'd read about it. All except JoAnn. She remained cynical. Once in a while when she thought no one was looking, she got involved in what Charlotte was saying and paid close attention. When it was over she said, "I might come back next week. I haven't decided yet."

Louisa, on the other hand, hugged Charlotte. "This is going to be wonderful. Thanks so much for doing this."

"My pleasure. See you all next week." As soon as she closed the door, she had a strong desire to call Pastor Gordon and let him know it went well since he'd been praying, but she thought that would be a bit strange. She decided to leave a message on the church answering machine instead, assuring him that he need not call her back.

CHAPTER FIFTEEN

Frank decided to pull out all the stops. Around midday on Tuesday, Charlotte answered a knock on her door. There stood the florist with the biggest bunch of roses she'd ever seen. As she exclaimed over them, the elderly delivery man said, "Yep that's the most I've seen someone order. Three dozen. Either you did something really great or you're much admired, young lady."

The note attached read, "To the most beautiful woman in the world. I can't wait until Thursday." Charlotte smiled like a woman who's just been given the keys to an enchanted kingdom. She searched for a vase, but none were big enough. Against her better judgment, she decided to ask Mrs. Bartholomew. Walking up to her front door, she stopped to pet Custer, who napped on the doorstep as if keeping watch. She thought it best to keep on the good side of Custer.

"Yes?" Mrs. Bartholomew answered so quickly that Charlotte felt pretty certain that she knew she was coming.

"Would you have a vase I could borrow?"

"Got flowers, huh?"

"Yes, I did. The trouble is I need a large vase. Do you have a really big one?"

"I've got every kind of vase imaginable. Come on in." Charlotte followed her to a hall closet. One entire shelf was filled with vases of all shapes and sizes.

"Wow. I never knew there were this many vases in the world." She reached out and pointed to a tall, bronze colored one. "This one looks like it would work."

Mrs. Bartholomew handed it to her. "It your birthday?"

"No, just something kind from a friend."

She nodded. "Frank, huh?"

Charlotte nodded and smiled. There were certainly no secrets from Mrs. Bartholomew. "Thanks for the vase. I'll take good care of it."

"You'd better." There was no hint of amusement. In fact, she seemed mad about something.

"Are you sure it's all right if I borrow it?"

Relaxing, she said, "Yes, go ahead. Take it." Charlotte left wondering what that was all about. "What are we going to do about this, Custer?" she asked. "She doesn't know her own mind."

The next day, Charlotte heard a knock on her door and saw a huge basket filled with chocolates of all varieties. It was so big she had trouble lifting it to bring it in. The note said, "Nothing could be sweeter than you." On Thursday she wasn't surprised, but still delighted, when she found a delicately sculpted china bowl filled with soaps and lotions. "I can't wait until tonight" was all the note said. Each gift made Frank seem dearer. She couldn't wait either.

At six thirty she made sure that her makeup was perfect, taking extra time to work on it. She used her favorite perfume and put her hair up, letting soft tendrils fall to her neck. The dress she wore was one of her favorites with tiny pearl buttons down the front and pleats that fitted it perfectly to her waist. He'd told her he was taking her to a restaurant they'd never been to before, full of atmosphere. She didn't know when she'd looked forward to a date more. She'd even called her mother to tell her about it.

At seven o'clock she was ready. He came about ten minutes late, but he arrived with another small bouquet of flowers and looked dashing in a new Italian cut suit.

"Charlotte, you look absolutely gorgeous. I hope there are no other women at this restaurant because they'll leave in tears when they see you."

"Oh Frank, that's ridiculous, but sweet. You're looking pretty good yourself."

He smiled, put an arm around her waist and led her out to his car. They chatted amiably on the way to the restaurant, about a thirty minute drive. He didn't ask her how her mother was, but so many people had asked her all week that she was glad not to talk about it again.

The restaurant was small and cozy, with candlelight and white tablecloths. He had special flowers ordered just for their table. She'd truly never been treated so royally. But when they sat down to talk, it seemed rather awkward. Frank obviously didn't want to talk about her mother or her church, and there wasn't much else that Charlotte was involved in. She asked him some questions about his work, but he said he didn't want to bore her to death. In the end they talked about their favorite restaurants and some of the best vacations they'd ever taken.

After dinner Frank led her outside. "The best thing about this restaurant is the location. See this path?" She nodded her head. "It leads to a pond. Do you want to follow it?"

"That sounds lovely."

He took her hand and led her down a path that had willows lining both sides, making a canopy of sorts to walk under. As they neared the water, they heard ducks quacking and frogs croaking to hasten the end of the day. They stopped at a stone bench which Frank brushed off with his handkerchief. "We wouldn't want you to get that beautiful dress dirty." When she sat down, he sat very close and began pointing out different things to see in and near the water. Soon his arm was around her. She felt so comfortable that without even thinking, she nestled into his arms, resting her head on his shoulder. They grew quiet and watched the sun begin to go down when Frank pulled her chin up so that her face was so close to his that she couldn't focus on it properly. He placed his lips on hers and pulled her into an embrace that took her breath away in more ways than one. It was wonderful to be kissed this way by a handsome man in this exquisite setting. But when he began to unbutton her top buttons, she grew alarmed. This was all wrong. It's not what she wanted at all. She pulled away and stood up quickly, "I'm sorry, Frank." She looked at his face and knew that things were not going to go well from here on out.

"What's wrong?"

"This is moving way too fast for me. I just need time to get to know you without getting involved physically."

"We're adults, for heaven's sake, Charlotte. We're not children."

"Exactly, so we should know that relationships are not built on kisses. It takes a lot more, and if we skip to the sex part, we'll get confused."

Frank looked mad enough to hit someone. She backed away a few steps. "You're the one who's confused." He pointed his finger at her, raising his voice as if accusing her in front of the town council. "You give one message with your body then another with your words."

Charlotte was afraid that he was right. "I'm sorry if I've mislead you. It's been an awful couple of weeks for me, and I guess I did want a knight in shining armor to sweep me out of the nightmare I'm in." She lowered her head and looked at the ground, "You tried to be that for me. I'm sorry I let you down."

Her contrite attitude made him calm down. He kicked a bush and scared a rabbit out of it which broke the tension and made them both laugh. "Maybe I pushed you a bit too, Charlotte. I think I'm a lot more ready to make a commitment than you are."

"I think that's true," she said so quietly that he almost didn't hear her. He wished he hadn't. He'd hoped he was wrong about that. "So what do we do from here?"

"Maybe we'd better not see each other for a while. After tonight I realize that I'm not going to be able to concentrate on anybody else but my mom."

He nodded, and they slowly walked back to the car. The ride home was silent, only the sound of the motor and the tires hitting the road.

The next morning Charlotte called Janice and asked if she would come over for lunch. "Sure. What can I bring?"

"Just yourself and your wisdom."

"I don't know if I have much of that, but I'll come anyway."

When she arrived, she saw the roses and said, "Wow. The florist must have had to close after delivering those." Charlotte gave her a sad smile and poured out the whole story of what went on between her and Frank. "I feel awful. He spent all that money and emotional energy on me."

Janice waved her hand as if batting a fly. "Don't worry about that. Frank has plenty of both to waste."

"Was I wrong?"

"Of course not. You were one hundred percent right. Don't you let him make you think otherwise."

"I'm such a poor judge of character, Janice. I should never be allowed to date. I mess up every time."

"That's just because you haven't found the right one yet. When you do, you'll know."

"Like you and Victor?"

Janice smiled as if she were sinking into a bath filled with rose petals. "Yes."

Charlotte felt relieved, as if she'd been given an absolution of her sins. "Well, I'm more determined than ever to remain single. I don't know why I get all these romantic notions in my head. If you hear me talking about any other man, just punch me really hard, okay?"

"Sure, that'll be fun." Janice grinned and Charlotte thought about how dear she'd become in such a short amount of time.

CHAPTER SIXTEEN

The summer passed like a dandelion seed in the wind. Charlotte spent it almost entirely with young girls. Misty and her friends continued to show up at least once a week and the high school girls completed the six week study that she had prepared. On the fifth session something wonderful happened. JoAnn continued to come each week but kept her attitude of skepticism. She'd been a leader among the girls, but now they began to distance themselves from her. Charlotte watched this with some alarm because she was afraid JoAnn would just quit coming and she knew in her heart that JoAnn needed this more than any of the girls.

On this particular night, they looked at what God had to say about saving sex until marriage. Charlotte had given the girls verses to read and asked them to come prepared. They all did except JoAnn. "I didn't have time" was her excuse. Throughout the study, she crossed her arms in front of her, frowning. Charlotte prayed for her the entire time but felt certain she was losing her for good. She concluded the study talking about the fact that God made the sexual relationship between men and women and that He delighted in it, but that it grieved Him when couples used it to manipulate each other or people perverted his beautiful plan into something hideous and grotesque. "There are examples of that all around us. Hollywood has made a fortune promoting it. But God has given us parameters to protect us. Marriage is that parameter." The girls were full of questions after that, and the study ended on a positive note.

Louisa suggested they all go out for ice cream afterwards. Charlotte told them to go ahead without her, and JoAnn said she wasn't interested. Marcie gave her a look that sent out daggers and several of the other girls rolled their eyes. "Don't look at me like I'm the town prostitute!" JoAnn yelled. "I just don't feel like going for ice cream." Charlotte jumped at this outburst, since that was the most JoAnn had said all evening.

The girls trickled out but JoAnn hung back. "Can I talk to you for a minute?"

"Sure."

"I believe every word you've said here, but I can't do it. I've gone too far away from God's principles to ever turn back. The damage is done, and it's hopeless for me."

"JoAnn," Charlotte said her name gently. "It's never too late. Think of the prodigal son, Mary Madeleine, the woman at the well. These are all people who'd turned their backs on God but came back. That's the beauty of Jesus Christ. It's never too late. Even the thief on the cross knew that."

She shook her head, "My boyfriend would never understand. He'd leave me so fast that my head would spin."

"Then he's not worth having. If he's only in the relationship for what he can get out of it, he's not the man for you."

JoAnn sat there with her head in her hands, rubbing her forehead as if to rid it of a terrible stain. And perhaps that is exactly what was going on. "You can see how the other girls think about me now. They won't want to be my friend, and I'll have no one."

"I don't know. I've gotten to know those girls pretty well the last few weeks." Charlotte fell silent thinking. "How about this...what if you share with them next week your commitment to change? Tell them you need their help to stand firm in your convictions. I think they'll be right with you."

JoAnn nodded. "I'd like to try that. Will you help me?"

"You bet," and Charlotte jumped up to hug her. "I can't wait to see how God is going to use this in your life,

JoAnn. You're going to be a new person." For the first time since the study began, JoAnn broke into a smile.

The next week, JoAnn came early so that they could pray and discuss what she should say. They decided to make it the first thing of the evening. When the study began, and JoAnn cleared her voice to speak, Charlotte thought it was the bravest thing she'd ever seen. The girls responded perfectly, surrounding JoAnn with hugs and promises of loyalty. When the study was over that night they all went for ice cream, treating JoAnn as if she were the virgin queen among them. It brought tears to Charlotte's eyes. She would miss the Monday night sessions more than she could say.

School started which ended the impromptu visits from Misty and her gang, and the Monday night study had ended. She was still involved with youth group and Wednesday night Bible study, but life lacked the momentum that she'd known when involved in so many things. The nice thing was that her schedule was open to see her mother. She went often for just a couple of days at a time. Her mom was still able to work part-time but had no energy for anything else. She'd lost her hair and relied on the wigs which made her look normal, except she was quite a bit thinner than usual.

Charlotte saw Frank every now and then, but it was awkward between them. He let her know that if she ever changed her mind that he'd be waiting, which brought her turmoil.

Pastor Gordon noticed that Frank didn't seem to be in the picture anymore, but Charlotte was very formal and stiff with him. He never got a word of encouragement from her, so he kept his distance. Their relationship remained polite but completely platonic. Something had been irrevocably stirred in Gordon through Charlotte though, making him question his long stance on being a bachelor. He remembered a girl he'd met in college who he hadn't heard from in years, so he struck up a correspondence with her. They now wrote regularly, encouraging each other in their professional, spiritual, and personal lives. It was a comfortable relationship. Gordon wondered sometimes if he liked it especially because it demanded little more from him than sitting down to write a letter every week or so.

Janice and Victor in the meantime were progressing at breakneck speed. She called Charlotte one evening. "I have the best news. Can you come over?"

"Right now?"

"Yes. It can't wait!"

Charlotte threw a coat on since the weather was getting quite chilly and drove to Janice's place. As soon as she walked in, Janice tore her coat off her and threw it on a nearby coat rack. "Sit down," she ordered. Charlotte sat, but Janice bounced, reminding Charlotte of Tigger in Winnie the Pooh. "He's asked me."

Charlotte knew perfectly well what Janice was talking about but she couldn't avoid having some fun. "Who's asked you what?"

"Victor's asked me."

"Oh, did he ask you to go to that play you've been wanting to see?"

"No, you ninny. He asked me to marry him!"

Charlotte broke into a big smile and threw her arms around Janice. "I'm so glad. It couldn't happen to a sweeter girl."

"Oh thank you, Charlotte. You'll be my maid of honor, won't you?"

"Really?" Charlotte was truly touched. "I'd love to. When's the wedding?"

"January 15th. It's a Saturday. We want an afternoon wedding. His daughter is going to be the flower girl, if we can get her to walk down the aisle." She clapped her hands, popping up and down on her tip toes. "It's better than I could ever have imagined it. Victor is absolutely perfect for me."

"I think he is. Let's go out to dinner tonight to celebrate."

"Oh, I'm sorry, I can't. Victor and I are going to go visit his grandmother and tell her. We have so many people to break the news to."

After visiting a few more minutes, Charlotte left feeling happy for Janice but blue for herself. The temptation to call Frank was enormous. Later that evening when she was eating her dinner alone, she thought that perhaps in her caution that she'd thrown out the baby with the bath water. Maybe Frank was the right person for her, but it had moved too fast. Maybe it was better to take a risk in a relationship she wasn't sure of than to be alone forever. She picked up the phone three times before she actually dialed the number, but when Frank answered on the third ring, she warmed to the task. "Hello," he answered abruptly as if expecting a business call.

"Hello, Frank."

"Charlotte! Wow, you're the last person I expected to call. Is everything all right?"

"Everything's fine. I was just wondering..." She paused, not at all sure how to proceed.

"Yes?"

"What would you think of starting over again from the very beginning?"

"You know I'd love to, Charlotte." His voice was soft and warm, giving her goose bumps.

"I'll need to take things really slow - just be friends, nothing physical, but get to know each other."

"I'd like that. I've thought a lot since our last meeting. I think that's one of the things that drove my first wife away. I always had my agenda instead of considering hers, and here I was doing it all over again. I want to do it right this time."

Charlotte's heart warmed to those words, "Thank you, Frank. I needed to hear that."

Frank cleared his voice, taking on the tone of a western cow poke, "Well, ma'am. How about if we go to the high school basketball game on Friday night? The team's pretty good this year, and I think some of your high school girls are cheerleaders."

Charlotte laughed. "I'd like that. How about if I meet you there and we sit together?"

"Sounds perfect."

"It does to me, too."

She hung up the phone feeling content. She was following her own advice to the young girls and it felt good.

CHAPTER SEVENTEEN

Charlotte had a blast. She saw Frank waiting just inside the entrance and waved to him. As it happened, Victor and Janice were there too, so they sat with them. Several of the girls from youth group saw her and bounded up to her. JoAnn came up and whispered in her ear, "I'm single and loving it. I didn't know how much I was missing." Charlotte hugged her, and the rest of the girls swept her away to buy popcorn.

The team won but not without a run for their money, so the evening was a success in every way. Afterwards, Victor asked them if they'd like to go out for coffee. Charlotte felt a little silly when she got in her car and Frank got in his, but she was glad they decided to do it this way. They seemed less like a couple to everyone observing and most importantly, to themselves.

As soon as they'd settled into the booth, Janice leaned forward, "I have news." Then she sat back with a satisfied grin on her face, waiting for the reaction. Charlotte bit, "Okay. Our curiosity is aroused. What's the news?"

"Pastor Gordon has a girlfriend." Her eyebrows arched and her smile grew bigger as she waited for her news to sink in.

This was the last thing in the world that Charlotte expected to hear and for some reason it made her feel sadder than anything had since she'd heard her mother had cancer. Frank, on the other hand, said, "That confirmed bachelor? I didn't think he knew what a woman was, other than to pray for her."

Victor laughed, "I have to admit. I'm surprised too. Who is she?"

"She's an old college friend. They've been writing for months now and decided it was time to get together. She's staying with Mrs. Donahue this weekend. I can't wait to meet her. She must be a saint for Pastor to notice her." She grinned and Charlotte forced a smile on her face.

Sunday morning dawned and Charlotte couldn't help but feel nervous about going to church because she'd have to meet "her." She'd started thinking of the woman in those terms, as an enemy to be faced. It made her mad when those thoughts crept in unbidden. "You are such an idiot. You should be glad for Pastor Gordon. Here he has a chance at happiness, and you would snatch it away from him. And God's given you another chance with Frank. How selfish can you be?" The fact was she could face it if Gordon remained single, but the idea that he might marry another woman made her feel like spitting. "God take this away from me."

And he did. She went to church and greeted Gloria with true warmth. She liked her very much. She was average height, had long blond hair and pleasant features. She particularly liked the manner with which she conducted herself. She met people well and had the ability to put them at ease right away. Charlotte couldn't have picked better for Pastor Gordon. When she was leaving the church she told him so as she shook his hand. "I like Gloria an awfully lot. It must be terrible for her having a whole church waiting to approve her, but she's handling it like a pro. I hope things work out between you."

Pastor Gordon gave her a strange little smile. "Thank you, Charlotte. That means a lot to me." He held her hand a little longer than necessary and seemed to let it go reluctantly as he studied her face. Evidently whatever he was looking for in her features he didn't find, so he changed the subject. "We'll see you at youth group tonight. Have a good afternoon." And she felt dismissed.

Gloria was gone by the time youth group rolled around. Pastor seemed exceptionally cheerful as he interacted with the kids. "I believe Gloria was good for him," Charlotte whispered to Mrs. Donahue, who frowned. Charlotte stared at her perplexed. "What's wrong?"

"I don't know. It's probably nothing." Then she turned to set out the snacks.

Gloria came often after that, every other weekend or so. She and Charlotte became good friends, and she began to stay with her once in a while instead of at Donahue's. Charlotte enjoyed her almost as much as Janice, but they were different as night and day. Gloria was serious and sober. Her greatest desire was to be of some great use for the Lord. Charlotte felt she'd be a perfect pastor's wife. She obviously respected Gordon a great deal and talked about him as if he were a ministry partner rather than a lover. Charlotte wondered if that was what a good relationship should look like.

The day finally came when Pastor announced in church that he and Gloria were engaged. Charlotte was shocked because Gloria was staying with her that weekend and hadn't mentioned a word of it. She thought of Janice's enthusiastic pronouncement of the same news and wondered at the difference. Talking to Gloria later in the day, she found out that they'd planned a July wedding since Gloria was a teacher and wanted to finish out the school year.

Christmas came and Charlotte went home to be with her mom. Margaret had finished her radiation treatment and was now starting her chemotherapy. She'd just decided that she'd have to quit work, which was a real blow. Charlotte helped her gather together some crafts to work on. Her mom used to crochet but hadn't for years. Now she decided to take it up again by making baby blankets and sweaters for the local pregnancy center. Mrs. Bartholomew had suggested it, and Charlotte's mom liked the idea a lot.

They also found out that one of the pregnant girls needed a place to stay and Margaret eagerly offered her home. She let the girl know that she'd pretty well have to fend for herself but at least she'd have a place to stay where she'd be dry and warm. She moved in two days before Christmas. Lyla, who was just seventeen, attended the local high school. She wanted to keep her baby but had no idea how she'd support it. Her mom kicked her out six months back, and she'd shuffled around to different friends' houses. Three months ago, she'd slept with her friend's brother and now carried his child.

Charlotte liked Lyla immediately. She had a certain grit that few girls her age had. Her plan was to finish high school by June. Her baby was due later that month, so she'd take the summer to be with her baby. Then in the fall she'd go to the community college to become a nurse. She'd found out that a local hospital would pay for her education if she worked for them. So after school every day, she volunteered at the hospital until they saw that she was worthy of being hired. Charlotte couldn't believe it. She'd never had that much determination in her life.

Christmas day had new meaning since Margaret brought a homeless, pregnant woman into her home. Lyla listened as Charlotte read the familiar story of another woman who'd sought shelter on this day two thousand years ago. "Mary's kind of like me," she said. "Except I certainly didn't have no angel tell me it was going to happen. Or the spirit of God, for that matter, didn't cause it. But the story is comforting just the same."

Lyla and Margaret acted like old chums. By the second day, Margaret insisted that Lyla read the Bible to her at night after dinner. She asked her to start with the gospel of John and Lyla, who'd never read the Bible before, was full of questions. Each evening became an investigative study that drew Lyla closer. By the time Charlotte left, she felt confident that God had put Lyla in her mother's home to introduce her to Him and to give her mother new purpose and joy. God rarely did anything for just one reason. She praised Him all the way home and felt surprised that the person she most wanted to share this story with was Pastor Gordon.

CHAPTER EIGHTEEN

The day of Janice's wedding dawned cold and blustery. Just a few nights before, there'd been a huge snowstorm and the sky threatened to repeat its performance. But by noon the clouds dissipated, and the sun broke through shimmering on the snow as if accentuating the happiness of the occasion. It seemed fitting to Charlotte that Janice's wedding day be cheerful looking.

She carried her dress over to the church, where they would get ready. Peeking into the sanctuary she sighed. Bouquets of pink roses, baby's breath, and white irises tied with big blue bows lined the five front pews. An arch covered with fresh vines and baby's breath stood at the altar. She picked up the program that had a photo of Victor's large hand under Janice's small one. It made her feel good inside.

Working her way into the room where they would change, she found she was the last to arrive. Janice had been so anxious that she'd come an hour early to make sure everything was perfect. Her dress could only be described as elegant. There were more beads and netting than Charlotte could have imagined would fit on one dress. Although their styles were opposite, Charlotte felt Janice's choice perfect for her. The bridesmaid dresses that she and Janice's younger sister wore were more subtle, thankfully. A shade of royal blue, they shimmered when the light hit them. Fitted at the waist with long sleeves that came to a point on the middle of her hand, she felt like a medieval princess. All she needed was a pointed hat, but instead she had a small amount of baby's breath worked into her hair as it was piled on the top of her head.

They'd had a lot of fun the night before at the rehearsal dinner, but now as the music began in the sanctuary her stomach hurt with anxiety. Laughter rang through the sanctuary as Victor's little daughter scattered flowers so meticulously that she stopped every few minutes when she dropped them. The tension eased and Charlotte breathed deeply. Before her turn came to walk down the aisle, she gave the bride one final hug. Janice's smile was so big that Charlotte thought her face must hurt. She turned around to begin the slow march forward, when she saw Frank in one of the back pews. He gave her a thumbs up, and she smiled back at him. Then her gaze faced the front of the church and she saw Pastor Gordon standing there. The look on his face was so startling that she almost stumbled.

a month ago, but with her mom's health problems and her work at church, she'd been a little slower than usual. She still made her deadline, so her editor found no problem with it.

After she finished a book, Charlotte always took a month off before she started another one. She found that she needed that time to let a plot simmer in her mind. Often she came up with an idea for her next book while she was working on the last one, but this time she'd drawn a blank. The only plot she could think of involved a minister. There was no way she could write that story.

So Charlotte worried about what she was going to do. The thought occurred to her that she should just go away to a beach somewhere and get out of all this snow, but she didn't want to go away when her mom's health was so unstable. She remembered a flyer she'd gotten in the mail about activities in the community. She pulled it out now and perused it, looking for anything that caught her interest. Her finger stopped at ballroom dancing. She'd always wanted to learn how to do that. Maybe Frank would try it with her. Then she went on until she saw that tryouts for the play "Cheaper by the Dozen" were being held this coming Thursday night. She'd loved the old movie as a kid and decided to go ahead and try out. She hadn't acted since high school but knew she had a dramatic flair.

That night she called Frank before going to Bible study. "What would you think of taking ballroom dancing lessons with me?"

He groaned so loud that she pulled the phone away from her ear. "Why don't you just ask me to get a root canal?"

"Oh, for heaven's sake, it's not that painful."

"Yes, it is. What if I asked you to take football lessons with me? How would you feel?"

She had to admit that she wouldn't like it a bit. "Okay, I get the point."

"No hard feelings?"

"No hard feelings."

"But I've got another idea you might like."

"What's that?"

"Every Friday night for six weeks, the ice skating rink is giving figure skating lessons. They're going to cover turns, skating backwards, skating on one leg, you know, stuff like that."

"And you want to do that?" Charlotte couldn't see how different that would be from dancing.

"Yea, I play hockey all the time. I thought it'd improve my game."

"Ah, it's all clear now. Actually, that sounds great. I'd love it."

"I'll sign us up then. See you there Friday at seven."

That went better than I would have imagined. I've got to give him credit; Frank's really trying.

The next night, she went to play tryouts at the community center. She wanted to read the part of the mother, but they said she was much too young, and gave her the part of the eldest daughter. The practices would be every Thursday evening and Saturday morning for the next three months, so suddenly her schedule was full to the brim. Mondays and Tuesdays were open for visits to her mom occasionally so it seemed just about perfect.

Friday night she drove to the ice skating rink which sat at the edge of town. She was amazed that such a small town had one, but evidently an Olympic medalist had come from Crispens Point years ago and left a large sum of money to keep the place open all these years.

She noticed Frank's car and waved to him once inside. He already had his hockey skates strapped on. The instructor wanted him to rent figure skates, but he'd insisted on sticking with the ones he had. Besides that, he'd talked a whole slew of his buddies into taking the class with him.

Five hulking men with silly grins on their faces stared at the instructor expectantly.

Besides Charlotte, three other women were there and two teenage girls. They all had figure skates on. Evidently it hadn't occurred to the women hockey players that they could get an edge by taking figure skating. Charlotte rented size eight skates and hoped they'd fit. She hadn't skated since being a teenager when she'd go to a nearby lake with her friend's family. Standing up, she remembered how insecure she was on this little blade of metal expected to hold her up. But once she got out on the ice to warm up, she stayed on her feet without falling although there were a few close calls. She couldn't imagine going backwards or skating on one leg. It was hard enough using two legs going forward! And so far, her method of stopping was gliding to a wall and bumping up against it.

To make matters worse, Frank skated around the rink two times to her every one. He was excellent at making quick stops and turned on a dime. She started to wonder if he just wanted to take this class to show off, but the instructor didn't seem impressed. He blew a whistle to get their attention and waved the group over to him. "Welcome to all of you. We're glad you could come. I can see that you are all at different levels, but hopefully the skills I'll be teaching you will be helpful to each of you." He then skated out into a twirl that intimidated everyone. "We're going to start with turns. Those of you who have never turned will learn the basics. Those who are proficient will learn to do what I just did." The hockey players all stared, dumbfounded.

He then proceeded to demonstrate to those who were morons (that's how it made Charlotte feel) how to do a simple turn to stop, slow themselves down, or change directions. He sent them out to practice while he concentrated on the men and the two teenage girls who seemed eager to learn. Charlotte actually picked up the basic skills pretty easily. No one had ever showed her before, and she enjoyed working at getting better each time. Out of the corner of her eye she watched Frank and the other guys. She began to giggle as they awkwardly worked their way around a circle, making it smaller each time. A few fell over and most looked like football players trying to be ballerinas. She started laughing so hard that she fell over herself and landed on a hip that bore a good size bruise for the next few weeks. But it didn't stop her fun.

When the evening was over she thanked Frank for suggesting one of the most entertaining evenings she'd had in months. He stuck out his lower lip and pretended to pout. "You weren't by chance laughing at me, were you?"

"Who, me?" and she batted her eyes like a southern belle.

Over all it had been a great week.

CHAPTER NINETEEN

Saturday morning after play practice, she called her mom. "How are you doing, O great one?"

"Pretty good, little girl. It's good to hear your voice."

"How's Lyla?"

"Whew. She's one strong-willed lassie. She's even got you beat."

Charlotte grew concerned. "Is she too much Mom?"

"Nope," she said strongly, so Charlotte knew it wasn't up for discussion. "Nothing of value is ever easy."

"Is she breaking your rules?"

"Probably, but not in front of me anyway. She follows my curfew and reads the scriptures to me, and lately she's been doing extra things I haven't asked her to do."

"Like what?"

"She did my laundry and folded it. And she even made dinner the other night. She asked me to teach her how to cook, so that's our latest project. She's pretty bad about doing her own dishes, though. I have to keep on her about that."

"So, you're still glad you took her in?"

"Absolutely. It was the right thing." And she knew her mom meant it. As long as she believed something was right, she'd go through hell and high water no matter what it cost her. But in this case, Charlotte felt that her mom was getting back as much as she was giving. God was gracious.

After she hung up with her mom, she wanted to call Janice because she knew she would be getting back from her honeymoon today. But after checking the clock, she realized it was too early, so put it off. She missed her a lot this week. She was just about to start a letter to an old friend when she heard a knock on the door. Gloria stood there with bag in hand. Charlotte's hand flew to her mouth, "Oh no. I forgot. Did you come earlier?"

Gloria smiled and nodded, "Don't worry about it. I just went over to see Gordon first instead. It's no big deal at all. He just needed to work on his sermon so I thought I'd try again. Is it going to work out okay? I feel like I'm an awful imposition."

Charlotte grabbed her and pulled her in. "Not at all. I love your visits. I was just wondering what I was going to do for the rest of the day. I'm between books, and that always throws off my routine."

Gloria laughed so quietly, it reminded Charlotte of a delicate fairy the size of Tinker Bell. "That throws me off too, but reading them, not writing them." She walked in and set her bag down.

"Would you like a cup of tea or something?"

"That would be lovely."

So they sat down in the kitchen and began to chat, "So, how are the wedding plans coming?"

"Oh fine. It's going to be really simple. I've decided to just buy a regular dress that I'll be able to use again. I'd hate to spend all that money on something fancy. My sister is picking out her own dress to stand up with me, so I don't have anything to do about that. By July there should be plenty of flowers in my mom's yard, so we'll pick a bunch for bouquets."

Charlotte smiled politely at this account and thought how practical Gloria was and how easy and carefree a wedding like that would be, but she knew in heart of hearts that she'd want a big wedding with all the trimmings. She wasn't sure whether she was right about that or not. "I heard the church women were planning a big reception. We have some of the best cooks in our congregation. I can't wait."

"Oh, I told them not to bother. A nice wedding cake will be fine. That's the one item that we'll order and pay for. Gordon seemed a little disappointed about that but after I talked to him, he could see my point."

This whole conversation was depressing Charlotte, so she changed the subject. "All this talk of marriage makes me think about some of my favorite heroines in classic stories. Who's your favorite heroine?"

"Oh my, there's really very few that I admire. My favorite books are biographies, often of single women. I admire their grit and determination." She paused for a sip of tea. "I guess if I have to pick one, I'd say Jane Eyre. She was so deserving. What about you?"

Charlotte struggled after that answer but decided to be honest anyway. "I have two. Elizabeth Bennet from *Pride and Prejudice*." Gloria nodded in agreement. "And Scarlett in *Gone with the Wind*." This was obviously too much for Gloria.

"How could you possibly admire Scarlett? Elizabeth I could understand although she cares too much about appearances to please me, but Scarlett? She's awful."

"I know. I think that's why I like her. She's what I think women often want to be; powerful and strong, yet extremely feminine." Gloria looked like she was about to say something so Charlotte interrupted her. "Now don't get me wrong. I don't think we should be like Scarlett, not at all." This seemed to mollify Gloria. "But I like reading about her a lot. You have to admit she's extremely interesting."

"I don't think I have to admit that at all. She's despicable."

Charlotte decided that east would never meet west in this case, so she changed the subject. "The parsonage is awfully nice. Will you do any redecorating when you move in?"

"Oh no, I'd hate to waste the church's money that way. It's fine." Gloria looked at her watch. "Oh my, an hour's gone by already. I need to run a quick errand then meet Gordon back at the church. We're going to do some hospital visits this afternoon."

Charlotte saw her to the door and felt guilty for her ungenerous thoughts toward her. Gloria was an excellent person who would add a lot to the whole community, but she couldn't help feeling a little sad for Pastor Gordon. She couldn't even sort out why she felt that way.

CHAPTER TWENTY

Charlotte finally got hold of Janice a few days later, "How was it?"

"Divine. The Bahamas are perfect. I'm sure that heaven will have a Bahamas section."

"What's it like coming home to motherhood?"

The dreamy tone of Janice's voice immediately changed. "Kind of a shock. I think I'm going to be bad at it. Gina doesn't listen to me at all, and I just want to be her friend. I hate the discipline part. I feel like crying each time I scold her."

Charlotte thought that the honeymoon was over. "I'll bet. It seems like it would be hard enough to adjust to marriage without throwing motherhood on top of it."

"Yea, I think that's why God let our courtship go so smoothly. He knew I'd need all the help I could get for part B."

"How are you going to cope?"

"The question is how is my mom going to cope? I've called her three times already today."

"Well, if you feel like you need a break, or just want company in the middle of it all, I'm pretty free."

"Thanks, Charlotte. That means a lot. Tomorrow I start back at the bank part-time, which I think will be good. Gina and I will get along better if we don't spend quite so much time together."

She didn't talk to her again until Bible study on Wednesday night. "You look great, Janice. What a lot of freckles you have after all that sun."

"I know. I'm hoping my freckles will grow so numerous that they'll look like a tan."

"How's motherhood going?"

"Pretty good. The part-time thing is helping a lot. I actually look forward to picking her up at one o'clock. Then she goes down for a nap after we've read five thousand books. After that, *Sesame Street* and *Mr. Rogers*. By then I've started dinner and she's wide awake and ready to play. I like it."

Victor interrupted. "Don't let her fool you. She's about ready to pull her hair out when I get home. Sometimes I think I've gotten there just in time before she's decided to run out into the street screaming." He said this with a grin on his face, so Charlotte assumed that they thought this was a normal way to adjust to their circumstances. She liked them both.

On Friday night, she once again headed for the ice skating lessons. She worried a bit about this lesson because they'd be learning to skate backwards. The instructor had demonstrated it for them last week, making it look as easy as walking. She couldn't even walk backwards. She'd never be able to do this.

Frank skated by her and grabbed her hand to twirl her around. She began to fall so threw her arms around him dragging him down onto the ice. They ended up in a pile laughing like preschoolers. The instructor told them that pairs skating wouldn't be until the last lesson which brought a titter of laugher from everyone.

The lesson began with the instructor showing them how to start with their skates pointing together at the toes. Then he demonstrated how to curve their skates out into an arch which propelled them backwards. Charlotte wobbled precariously but she stayed on her feet as she brought her skates back in. She felt a great sense of victory as if she'd just landed a triple Lutz and diligently practiced the rest of the night until she covered half the rink before having to stop so she wouldn't fall.

Afterwards a group decided to go out to one of the bars. Frank looked at her with a question in his eyes, obviously wanting her to go. But she looked over at the high school girls and shook her head no. He caught the cue and smiled and waved as they left. She walked over to the girls to chat. "You girls are doing really well out there. I'd give a lot to have your grace."

"Aren't you the romance writer?"

Oh know, here it comes. "Yes, I am."

"We're friends with JoAnn. She's like a new person since she met you."

Charlotte was embarrassed that tears came to her eyes. She brushed them away quickly. "Thanks for telling me that. It means a lot."

The other girl who hadn't spoken yet said, "Would you repeat that class you taught? There's a bunch of us that would like to come."

"Of course. I'd love to. How about I give you my number, and we'll work out the details later."

"Thanks! We'll call."

It happened that the only time they could meet was Sunday afternoon which made Charlotte's Sundays rather busy. But a few of the girls came with her to youth group afterwards which surprised Charlotte. This group of girls was quite different from the last. The first group had a church background and was pretty familiar with the scriptures, but most of these girls had never stepped foot in a church and all of them demanded proof of the things she was saying. These sessions lasted twice as long with many more questions and a few dropped out after the first one, but the rest stayed and were growing. After a few weeks, Pastor Gordon pulled Charlotte aside before youth group. "Charlotte, I want to thank you for all the work you're doing with these girls. Their lives are being transformed because of you. I want to apologize for every suspicious thing I ever said about you."

His eyes held such warmth that she wanted to hug him, but she knew that would be inappropriate so she simply said, "Thank you, Pastor. That means a lot coming from you."

Two weeks later one of the girls came to Charlotte's door an hour before the group met. "Could I talk to you for a minute?"

"Sure, Carrie, come on in. Have you eaten lunch?"

The girl held her stomach and made a face. "No thanks. I don't feel much like eating these days."

Charlotte frowned but opened the door so she could step in out of the cold. "What can I do for you?"

"I have a problem. I haven't wanted anybody to know, but I feel like I can tell you. You've got to promise that you won't tell anyone." The girl looked at Charlotte fiercely, as if swearing her to a blood oath.

"I'll not tell anyone if I feel you aren't in some kind of danger. That's the best promise I can give."

The girl relaxed and said, "I'm bulimic." She stared at Charlotte waiting for a response.

Charlotte was actually surprised. She was sure she was going to tell her she was pregnant. "I see. How long has this been going on?"

"About a year, but it's getting now so that my stomach hurts all the time from so much vomiting and I've started to bleed down there," she pointed to her lap, "from all the laxatives."

"You need to get to a doctor, you know."

"I know, but I can't go here. Everyone in town would know if I go here."

"Have you talked to your mom about it?"

"No, she'd just yell at me."

"I can't take you to a doctor without your mom's permission. How about if I come over to your house tomorrow night and we talk to her together about it?"

The girl sat there looking trapped. Finally she said, "Okay. But you've got to tell her. I can't say a thing."

"That will be fine. I'll come over after dinner."

The next night Charlotte's own stomach hurt at the prospect of facing Carrie's mom. She didn't even know her, after all. As soon as she was sure they'd be finished with dinner, she drove to their house and knocked on the door. A young boy with two teeth missing answered it. He stood there looking at her without saying anything. Charlotte finally broke the silence. "Is your mom here?"

"Mom!" he yelled then disappeared down the hallway, leaving the door wide open. A plump woman in blue jeans and a sweatshirt walked up with a dishtowel in her hand. "I don't want whatever you're selling and I don't have time to take any political surveys or sign any petitions."

"I'm not doing any of those things. I'm here because Carrie asked me to come. She wants me to help her discuss something with you."

"If this is about going to space camp, I'm going to skin that girl alive. I told her we can't afford it."

"No, this isn't about space camp. May I come in?" She was starting to shiver standing on the doorstep.

The woman nodded but continued to regard her with suspicion. She turned her head and yelled "Carrie!" so loud that Charlotte jumped. "Go ahead and sit down." Charlotte chose a place on the sofa, and the mother sat in an overstuffed chair that had seen better days. Carrie walked in and sat down on the sofa next to Charlotte. She looked like she wished she could have disappeared into the cushions. "What's this about, Carrie?"

"Mrs. James, your daughter has an eating disorder."

For a large woman, she leapt to her feet quite nimbly. "What? Who are you anyway, and what do you think you're doing telling nonsense about my daughter?"

Charlotte remained seated and tried to keep her voice calm. "I don't blame you for being upset. I'm a perfect stranger to you. Your daughter has been coming to my house for a study on Sunday afternoons."

The woman squinted her eyes as if seeing Charlotte for the first time. "You're that romance writer, aren't you? What kind of silly stuff are you telling these girls?"

"Carrie has been making herself throw up, and she's been using laxatives for about a year. She's in bad enough shape now that she needs to see a medical doctor."

"Well, why didn't you say so?" She looked at Charlotte as if she were involved in a conspiracy with her daughter. "We'll go see Doc Morgan tomorrow."

Carrie spoke up. "No, Mom. I can't go see him. Everyone in town would know."

Her mom looked at her for the first time, "Why didn't you tell me instead of going to a perfect stranger?"

"You yell at lot, Mom."

Her mother blushed bright red, "I only yell because I love you. You and Timmy are my life. I sweat blood for you two. I've always told you to come to me with trouble."

"I was scared. It was easier to tell Charlotte." She then looked at her mom with pleading in her eyes, reminding Charlotte of a puppy she had once. She'd almost yelled these words, but now her tone became soft. "I'm really sick, Mom." Her eyes teared up and Mrs. James came over and threw her arms around her.

"It's going to be all right, honey. We'll get you some help. My HMO covers a doctor in Carlston. I'll call him tomorrow, and we'll get you in to see him."

The tears came in earnest now and Charlotte decided it was time to slip out. Mrs. James stopped her, "I'm sorry I almost bit your head off. I can see you just wanted to help. We're much obliged."

Charlotte nodded and slipped out the door.

CHAPTER TWENTY ONE

Ice skating ended and play practice became more intense, but Charlotte loved it. She'd made new friends, and even had a group over for dinner one night before rehearsal. She and Frank still saw each other regularly and she wondered where their relationship was going. She knew he was just waiting for a word from her but she couldn't quite give it.

Their dates had taken an interesting turn. They did a lot of sledding, snowmobiling, and skating, which almost always put them with a crowd so they rarely had a moment alone. But now the snow had melted and winter was winding down. They needed to find a new avenue for their energies. They both started including each other in things they had to do anyway, which worked out rather well because they now had a friend to invite along. During one of these events, Charlotte met Shari, Frank's ex. She'd just moved back into town and looked great. Charlotte could see what Frank saw in her. She was cute and lively, full of humor. They seemed to click as if Shari had never been gone.

A few weeks later, Charlotte got a call from Frank. "Charlotte, I don't know how to say this."

"You and Shari are getting back together."

She wished she could see his face. "How in the world did you know that?"

"I knew the night I met her. You guys are meant to be with each other."

"I can't believe it. Are you mad?"

"Not at all. It's been a great time, Frank, but we both know it wasn't going to work out between us."

"You're the greatest, Charlotte. I don't think Shari would have taken me back if it wasn't for you. You taught me a lot." His voice had sounded excited up to this point, but now he grew sober, "I hope you find someone too."

"Thanks, Frank. But I'm doing fine."

They hung up, and Charlotte cried. Not because Frank wasn't available anymore, but because she felt lonely. She was glad she had the play.

The play was a rousing success. Her mother came to watch with Lyla and sat with Mrs. Bartholomew. All her high school girls were in attendance, and she was touched that many of the church people came, including Pastor Gordon. He beamed a huge smile, clapping enthusiastically when she came out for the final bow with the rest of the cast. His smile filled her with warmth.

Her mother was waiting for her when she came out of the dressing room. It alarmed her that she was leaning heavily on Lyla. "It's been too much for you tonight, Mom. Let's get back to the house."

"I loved every minute of it, but I must admit I'll be glad to see a bed."

When they got up the next morning, Margaret made an announcement. "Now that your play is over and you are a little freer, I'd like to propose that we go to London." Charlotte and Lyla looked at her as if she'd suggested they form a band a make a world tour.

"Mother, what are you thinking? You don't have enough energy to do all the normal stuff."

"My whole life I've planned on going to London, so I'm going. You two can either come with me or stay here."

Lyla looked at Charlotte to see what she would say. All Charlotte got out was "Mother" again before Margaret interrupted her. "Now, little one, I'm not being unreasonable. I checked into a tour package that allows me to do as much or as little as I want. I'd like to see the Tower of London, the changing of the guard and the Royal Kew Gardens. We also would get tickets to “Les Miserables” on Saturday afternoon. We'd fly over there on a Monday and come back on a Sunday. You girls can shop or whatever while I'm resting. I wouldn't do any more than I do now. I don't have another chemo injection for several weeks. What do you think?"

Charlotte looked at her mom and saw that look that refused defiance. "When would we leave?" she asked with a smile.

Margaret smiled back with a look of relief. "Next Monday."

Lyla looked at first one then the other, "Holy moly, I'm going to London!"

Fortunately Margaret had planned this as soon as she found out she had cancer, so she'd applied for passports for her and Charlotte. Lyla actually had one already because she'd taken a trip to South America a few years ago to stay with a relative. The week flew by as they made the final preparations, and Monday afternoon they drove to the airport.

The flight took all night because of the time change, and they arrived in London at 7:00 a.m. England was already in the full bloom of spring, so they delighted at the many daffodils surrounding the airport and the green grass awaiting them. At home it was still brown and only a few crocuses forced their way through the frozen earth. The tour company arranged for them to be picked up and taken to their hotel. By the time they got there, Margaret was in desperate need of a nap. "You go to sleep Mom, and we'll bring you back some lunch."

Charlotte and Lyla roamed around the general vicinity of the place, taking in the centuries-old architecture. Their hotel was on Russell Square so they spent some time sitting in the park. Although overcast, it wasn't raining and the temperature was at least in the fifties. It was quite pleasant. Finally they found a little pub down a side street and looked at a menu. Lyla ordered fish and chips and Charlotte a ploughman's lunch. They decided to start their journey with authentic English food. "So what's it like living with Mom?"

"She's great. If my mom had been like her, I'd be a different person. You're one lucky woman."

"I know it. I thank God all the time for that."

"I mean, how many women diagnosed with cancer would take a trip overseas? She's crazy in a really cool way."

"Yes, she is," Charlotte laughed and she looked around her. "Maybe I'll make my next book set in London."

"I read one of your books."

"You did?"

"Yea." She didn't say anything else so Charlotte was afraid to ask.

"And?"

"It was okay."

Charlotte smiled. "I can tell you really loved it."

"Oh, I think you're a good writer and all. It's just not the kind of book I like."

"That's fair enough; we all have different tastes."

"Good. I'm glad I got that off my chest. It's been bothering me. You're not mad?"

"Not a bit. It takes a lot more than that to make me mad." They fell silent and ate a while, but Charlotte had to admit it did bother her. She would very much like to have Lyla's respect.

After lunch they took a lunch up to Margaret. She was just waking up from a nap, looking refreshed. "Our cruise down the Thames starts in just an hour. We need to get on the subway and go."

"Eat a bite first, Mom. We've got plenty of time."

Charlotte was surprised when her mom actually sat down and ate. After polishing off a good bit, she got up and said, "Let's go."

Fortunately the station was close to the hotel so they got on a train and made it to the boat just as boarding began. They settled into their seats as Margaret let out a deep sigh. "I can't believe I'm going down the Thames. I've read English novels my entire life and now I'm finally here. This is the life." Charlotte marveled at her mother's spirit.

The next day they toured the Tower of London. It took most of the morning and although Charlotte pushed Margaret in a wheelchair, the excitement still wore her out but in a happy way. They had a colorful Beefeater tour guide who made England's history seem like a bloody mess. All of them marveled at seeing a structure that was almost a thousand years old.

In the afternoon while Margaret napped, Charlotte and Lyla shopped. They enjoyed the street musicians and stopped often to listen or to watch a mime do something clever. Neither of them bought anything because Lyla had no money and Charlotte didn't see anything she couldn't live without.

That evening Charlotte managed to get tickets to “Ninety Minute Shakespeare”, a hilarious comedy where three young men act out all of Shakespeare's plays in ninety minutes. They all laughed until their sides hurt. The next day took a toll on Margaret so Charlotte and Lyla spent the day at the British Museum which was nearby while Margaret read and rested in the park.

Thursday they went to Westminster Abbey and Charlotte was delighted that while they were there a woman came on the loudspeaker and prayed for all writers. Friday was the Kew Gardens. It rained, but not enough to stop them. She thought her mother liked it best of all.

Saturday, after *Les Miserables,* they began to pack to go home since their flight left early the next day. As they sat talking about their week, Margaret said, "This was the greatest. I've seen all the things I've heard about my whole life, even Drury Lane and Buckingham Palace. Charlotte got ideas for her next novel and Lyla can tell her baby that she's been to London." She got up, gave them each a hug and said, "Thanks, girls."

"Thank you," they both chimed in at once.

Charlotte sat on the plane ride home thinking about all the wonderful things they'd done in one short week. She was startled when the thought went through her mind that she wanted to tell Pastor Gordon all about it. She'd thought of him often this week as they saw different sights. He was quite a history buff and she knew he'd love it here. “What's wrong with you?” she thought. “He's practically married.” Then she remembered something her mother told her years ago. "You can't keep a bird from flying over your head, but you can keep him from building a nest in your hair." She decided then and there that she'd chase that bird to kingdom come if it came close again.

CHAPTER TWENTY TWO

A week or two after Charlotte came back she noticed that things were dark at Mrs. Bartholomew's house. Worried about her, she walked over to check things out. After Charlotte rang the doorbell twice, Mrs. Bartholomew swung the door open. She looked awful. Her hair hadn't been combed and she still had her robe on even though it was late afternoon. "Mrs. Bartholomew, are you feeling all right?"

The elderly woman blinked at Charlotte as if trying to make out who she was. Finally she said, "I'm fine." Then she turned her back and walked away from the door, leaving it wide open. Charlotte followed her in which Mrs. Bartholomew didn't seem to notice at first. When she sat down in her easy chair, Charlotte sat down across from her. "Do you need to see a doctor?"

"I told you I was fine," she snapped. Then as if realizing for the first time that Charlotte was sitting in her living room, she added, "What are you doing here anyway?"

"I thought I'd come visit."

Mrs. Bartholomew looked at her through squinted eyes as if trying to figure her out, but she said nothing and the silence grew between them the way kudzu takes over a tree. Charlotte felt as though something was out of place. She looked around the room trying to put her finger on it when it hit her, "Where's Custer?"

No sooner were the words out of her mouth when the old woman put her head into her hands and wailed so loudly that for a moment Charlotte thought she was in physical pain. But then she heard her voice as she rocked back and forth, "Dead, dead, dead. Everyone dies and leaves me alone." The gut wrenching sobs that tore from her throat caused Charlotte to fight tears as well. She jumped up and wrapped her arms around the frail little woman rocking with her as a mother would comfort a child. "Not everyone," she whispered, "I won't leave you. I'll stay." Mrs. Bartholomew clutched her as if she were hanging on a cliff and would fall off if Charlotte let go, and perhaps that was the case.

For a long time the two women stayed there in each other's embrace. Charlotte stroked her hair and muttered, "It's going to be all right, it's going to be all right." Neither of them knew if that was true but it helped them both for Charlotte to say it. After a while Charlotte asked, "Can you tell me what happened to Custer?" She almost regretted asking because the tears began to flow in earnest again.

"I don't know. I just found him lying out at the bushes. I tried to pump his little heart the way they do on those doctor shows on TV, but it was too late. Too late."

Charlotte decided that something had to be done. "I tell you what. We're going out to breakfast tomorrow to celebrate Custer's life. He had a long, full one and we're going to order omelets and reminisce. I'll come at get you at eight o'clock."

"You must think me a silly old fool."

"I do not! I think you are a woman who loves deeply. A companion of fifteen years is nothing to sneeze about. But I don't think it's good for you to mope around like this. I want you to get up tomorrow and fix your hair, and put on that pastel flowered dress you look so nice in. Okay?"

Mrs. Bartholomew nodded. Charlotte rose to leave. "How about if we order pizza and watch a movie tonight? I know you like The African Queen, so I'll bring it over and we'll chum around like old school girls. What do you say?"

The elderly woman seemed to be herself again, "I'd like that." She paused a moment, then added, "Thank you, Charlotte."

"You bet. You'd do the same for me." And Charlotte knew she would.

Breakfast was a lot of fun. Mrs. Bartholomew came out of her house looking like she was going to high tea. Even though they only went to The Junction, she enjoyed every minute of it. She hadn't been out to eat in years. They ordered more than they could possibly eat but it gave them an excuse to sit there for a long time. She told Charlotte stories about Custer that made her laugh so hard that they both had trouble eating. When a waitress said, "You two are having way too much fun over here," they both giggled as if sharing a secret.

When they finished eating, Charlotte announced that they had one more stop to make. As she headed into the country, Mrs. Bartholomew asked, "Where are you taking me?"

"You'll see."

They drove quite a ways until they came to a farmhouse with a large barn. There were several dogs in a fenced in yard and a woman in overalls who looked as if she'd been doing chores. Charlotte walked up to her and said, "I'm the one who called about the kittens."

"Oh yes, they're out in the barn. Come with me."

"Now wait a minute." Mrs. Bartholomew began looking as if she'd hit Charlotte if she were given a chance. She started to complain. "No one can take Custer's place. I can't just get another one, and that is that. I thought you understood." Charlotte ignored her as they both followed the woman to the barn. "Unless you've had a pet, you can't possibly know what it's like to lose one. You don't just go out and get one the next day. Why I..." Her prattle of words stopped abruptly as the woman placed a little gold bundle of fur in Charlotte's hands.

"Look at this face. This poor baby needs a home. You wouldn't let him grow up to be a wild barn cat, would you?" The kitten was squirming and mewing pitifully in Charlotte's grasp.

"Oh for heaven's sake. You don't even know how to hold a kitten." She grabbed it out of Charlotte's hand cradling it in her arms. The tiny thing immediately began purring. "They're like babies. You have to know how to comfort them." She started petting it, looking it over in the eyes, behind the ears. "It's kind of a scruffy looking thing. Needs some fresh meat and a good brushing too. Custer kind of looked like this one when he was a kitten. I had to fatten him up, too."

Charlotte smiled, "Well, what do you think?"

Mrs. Bartholomew sighed as if she were doing a great deed, "I guess I can't just leave it here. The poor little thing needs a home."

"We'll take him," Charlotte said to the woman with a smile.

"That's good. It's always hard to find a home for the kittens. It looks like Mustard there will get a good one."

"Mustard, is that what he's called?" Mrs. Bartholomew narrowed her eyes.

"That's what we call him, but you can name him whatever you want."

"I like that. Mustard's a good name. Kind of tangy, a little bit of spice. A cat should have a name to live up to. Yes, I like it very much."

On the way home, Mustard fell asleep, curled in a tiny ball on Mrs. Bartholomew's lap. "How did you know to go there?"

"I looked in the paper for kittens, and then called the three places that advertised them until I found one that had a tiger kitty. I just knew it was going to work out."

"You took a big chance, you know. I could have flatly refused the kitten."

Charlotte smiled, "I don't think it was such a big chance."

Mrs. Bartholomew smiled back.

CHAPTER TWENTY THREE

On April Fool's Day, Gloria broke her engagement to Pastor Gordon. He announced it from the pulpit the next Sunday. "Many of you have come to love and appreciate Gloria as she has spent many weekends here, often in your homes. I hope that we can continue to care for her as she is following the call that God has placed on her life to go into the mission field. At a conference we both attended, she went to a seminar about a need for teachers at a school in Zambia. She knew immediately that this was for her. As you know, Gloria doesn't do anything rashly, but she has never wanted to go anywhere more clearly than she wants to go to Zambia. Therefore, we thought it best to break our engagement." It had been so quiet in the congregation that you could hear a mouse squeak, but now there were murmurings all around.

"I don't want you to pity me in any way. I'm in complete support and agreement with Gloria, and I hope we can encourage her in this endeavor. I wanted to announce this to you myself so that rumors would not swirl around, so please put this information aside and we'll continue with our worship service."

People talked for weeks about how brave their young pastor was as he made this announcement, but only he knew in his heart the relief he felt. He'd come to believe that he would have had a good life with Gloria, and that she'd be a great asset to his ministry, but somewhere along the line, he knew it wasn't enough. The defining moment had been when he saw Charlotte walking down the aisle in Janice's wedding. What he felt for Gloria could not compare to what he felt for Charlotte. Although he thought it unlikely that he'd end up with Charlotte, he knew he could never marry until he felt that kind of passion for a woman. When Gloria told him about her desire to go to Zambia, he felt like doing cartwheels but of course, he couldn't show it. It bothered his conscience when he heard the reassurances of how noble he acted under the circumstances.

He also thought that he should let a decent interval go by and then ask Charlotte out. She didn't seem to care for him, but he'd never know until he tried. For the time being, he'd wait.

Charlotte had mixed feelings about Pastor Gordon's announcement. She felt sad for him because she knew what it was like to be rejected. It also brought her turmoil because when he was engaged, it acted as a buffer for her emotions. Now that he was free again, it would be harder to discipline her mind, especially since she saw him twice a week every week.

To make matters worse, they were thrown together on a youth group outing. The Donahues planned a three-hour canoe trip down the river. When everyone arrived, students were assigned to different canoes. As it turned out, Gordon and Charlotte were put in the same canoe. Charlotte would have declined if there was any way she could think of getting out of it, but there seemed no gracious way. So the two of them strapped on their life jackets and climbed into each other's company for the next three hours. Pastor Gordon was delighted, but he noticed that Charlotte looked like a scared rabbit about ready to bolt, so his heart sank. It was clear she didn't want to be with him.

They made light talk as they dipped their paddles into the water. Every now and then a canoe of students would come by theirs to splash water at them or threaten to tip them over, but otherwise it was just the two of them. After they'd been paddling about an hour, Pastor got up his courage, "I've heard that Frank has gone back to Shari." Since he was behind her, he couldn't see her face, which she was thankful for. "Yes," she said a little too abruptly, "I guess neither you nor I are very lucky at love."

Her tone was sad, making him feel miserable. “She was really hurt by him,” he thought. “I'd like to wring his neck.” But aloud he said, "Not necessarily. Maybe we just haven't found the right person yet."

Charlotte laughed harshly, "Or maybe we need to accept that being single is the state we are to stay in."

Her words hurt him because they sounded so final. He thought it best to change the subject. "You know, I am continually amazed at your talents. You are a fine writer, you can assemble a very good Bible study, and you are an excellent actress. Is there anything you can't do?"

“Why is he doing this to me?” she thought.

"Apparently I'm not very good with the opposite sex."

Gordon grimaced as he realized that the subject change hadn't been complete. He tried again. "How is Janice doing?"

This question perked Charlotte up, "She's doing very well. Being an instant mom is quite a challenge and she has her frustrations, but I'm proud of her. She's doing great."

They continued on with small talk the rest of the journey. By the time they pulled their canoe out of the water, Pastor Gordon was certain that Charlotte wanted nothing to do with him.

Charlotte, on the other hand, wondered if Gordon had more than just a spiritual interest in her, but the thought scared her to death. She'd spent so much energy ignoring her feelings for him that she didn't dare entertain them for a moment. Her feelings were like a young bull that's been in a pen all spring and is suddenly released. It may be nice to let him out, but who knows what kind of damage he would cause. No, it was too dangerous. She must keep her emotions at bay at all costs.

The next Monday, Janice called Charlotte to see if she'd like to go with her to take Gina to the park for a picnic lunch. It was a perfect spring day, seventy-five degrees, sunny, with just a light breeze. Charlotte jumped at the chance. Janice picked her up at one thirty and they drove the short distance to the park. Charlotte loved this place with its rickety bridge, weeping willows, and old band shell that had gingerbread galore. At this time of year spring beauties covered the ground around them. As soon as Gina was unstrapped from her seat, she took off running for the swings laughing as if she knew a secret joke. "You'd think she spent all day in a cage," Janice quipped as they hurried to keep up with her. "Only a few pushes on the swing, Gina, then we need to eat a bite. I know you've already had your lunch but Mommy and Aunt Charlotte are hungry."

Charlotte watched with affection as Janice put the little girl in the swing and pushed her as she yelled, "Higher, Mommy, higher!" Finally, she seemed content to play in the sandbox while Charlotte and Janice spread their lunch on a nearby picnic table. "You seem like you've been a mom forever, Janice. She obviously loves you."

"I love her too. People always talk about a mother's heart, and I never understood it until now. I'd fight lions for her and if anyone tried to hurt her, I'm sure I could rip them apart with my bare hands." Charlotte chuckled as she thought of diminutive Janice tearing someone apart. Suddenly Janice changed the subject. "What do you think of this business with Pastor and Gloria?"

Charlotte felt annoyed. She was having such a good time. Why did everyone want to talk about that all the time? "I think they're doing the right thing."

"Me too. You know, I never felt right about the two of them as a couple, just like I never felt right about you and Frank."

"Wow, you ought to go into the business. You know, screen couples and save them a lot of time."

Janice laughed. "Oh, I've been wrong as much as I've been right. I don't want that responsibility." She took a bite of sandwich and they both looked around, enjoying the loud whistle of a wren and the croaking of some toads near the pond. "What about you and Pastor?"

Charlotte felt like her best friend had just stabbed her with a knife. It was as if she'd been wearing all these clothes to cover up a wart and Janice had just ripped them off, revealing it to the world. She took another bite so she wouldn't have to answer for a minute. "What would make you say something crazy like that?"

"I don't know. I just think you two would be perfect for each other, that's all."

"Well, get that out of your mind. It would never work."

"Why not?"

"There are things even you don't know about me, Janice."

The harsh way Charlotte said this hurt Janice's feelings. "Maybe it would do you good to tell them."

"Believe me, you don't know what you're talking about. It's best left alone."

"Do you like him?"

"It doesn't matter whether I like him. I mean it, Janice. Drop it."

This was the first time that a wall had come between the two friends and at the moment it seemed impenetrable. Janice ate the rest of her sandwich in two bites, hurrying off to push Gina on the swing.

"Okay, are you going to tell me up front, or are you going to leave me to guess what's bothering you?"

Charlotte jumped up to straighten a picture that hung crooked on the wall. "It's nothing really. I just needed a change."

"Why, because life is so stressful in Crispens Point?" she said with a smirk.

"Very funny. As a matter of fact, it is stressful, just a different kind of stress. Well, I've got to unpack." And she slammed the door as she went out to the car.

Margaret shook her head and looked at Lyla, rolling her eyes. "I guess she doesn't want to talk quite yet. Charlotte can be infuriating sometimes."

"Aren't we all, Ms. Fyne, aren't we all."

"Never a truer word was spoken." They smiled and Lyla stood up, which took some effort since she was growing in size daily.

"I've got homework to do, and then I'm off to work. Need me to do anything?"

"No, you go ahead with your stuff. I'm fine."

Charlotte came back in carrying so much that it looked like armor around her. Her mother wondered if that wasn't symbolic of what was going on inside. When she'd finally unpacked all her things, she started on dinner.

"I'm not that hungry, honey. Why don't you just sit down and visit?"

"There'll be plenty of time for that later. I like cooking. You've got chicken breasts in here, so I'll do a stir fry."

Margaret sighed and shook her head.

After dinner, Charlotte found plenty of other things to do, from dusting to starting a load of laundry. Margaret finally gave up on her and went to bed.

The next morning Charlotte had breakfast ready and started out the door as soon as Margaret got up. "I'm going shopping for some clothes. There's no place to shop around Crispens Point. I'm in desperate need of some new pants. I'll be back this afternoon. After she left, Margaret went into Charlotte's room. There were at least a dozen pairs of pants hanging in her closet.

She got home just in time for dinner. "I brought home a pizza and a movie," she said as if it were an idea no one had ever thought of before.

"Did you find some pants?"

"What? Oh, no, I didn't. You know how hard it is for me to find something that fits. I must have tried on three thousand pairs."

They ate pizza in silence and Margaret fell asleep before the video ended.

The next day Charlotte again left, saying she had to do research at the library for her latest book. She returned in time for dinner again, but then went out for a long walk. On the fourth day, Margaret had enough. When Charlotte announced she was going for a drive, she put her foot down. "Have a seat, Charlotte."

"What?"

"You aren't going for a drive just yet. We need to talk."

"I don't feel like talking, Mom. Talking never gets me anywhere. It makes me think too much."

"So, you're going to go through life without thinking anymore?"

"No, just not for a while. I need some time."

"Time for what?"

"Just time! Why can't you let it be at that?"

"Because however you think you're handling this, it's not working. I've never seen you more miserable and if you're going to use my home as a way of escape, forget it. I'm not going to let you."

Charlotte flushed red as she raised her voice, "Why do you always have to meddle? Why can't you just let me live my life?" As soon as she said these words, she regretted it. Her mother's face mirrored more pain than in all her battles with cancer. She felt thoroughly ashamed of herself. "I'm sorry, Mom. I'm acting just like I did in high school. You shouldn't have to put up with that."

Margaret recovered quickly. "You're nothing like you were in high school. But please, Charlotte. Don't shut me out."

Charlotte put her hands over her face and began to cry, "I don't know what's wrong with me. I keep messing everything up."

"Is this about Frank? I didn't know you cared for him that much."

She pulled herself together, drying her eyes and blowing her nose. "No, this isn't about Frank. He was never more than a friend."

"Is there someone else?"

Charlotte nodded her head.

"Who? You've never mentioned another man."

The tears threatened again, so Charlotte forced out her words, "That's because the man I really care about, I have no hope of a relationship with."

"Why?" Margaret looked truly bewildered.

"Because he would never want me. Not if he knew."

"Who is this man, Charlotte?"

"Pastor Gordon."

"Pastor Gordon! Why, he's wonderful. Why wouldn't you want to date him?"

"Mother, think about it. Think about my past. What kind of minister's wife would I make?"

Margaret looked angry, "A good minister's wife. Not perfect, but good. Christ came to forgive sinners; that should be the hallmark of what Pastor Gordon believes." Charlotte didn't look up so Margaret continued, "Has he shown interest in you?"

"He just asked me out before I came here. That's what's so frustrating. I think he does like me."

"Then be honest with him. Give him a chance."

Charlotte's pain was so intense that it felt physical. "I don't think I can stand it, Mother. I couldn't even keep John's love and respect. How could I expect to keep Gordon's? I can't live through another rejection."

"I see." Her mother looked thoughtful as she pulled an afghan over her legs. "So, it's okay to get involved with Frank, someone you don't respect so much, because he would've been less likely to reject you."

Charlotte hated that. Her mother could always see through her. She closed her eyes and repeated, "I don't think I could stand it. I already love Gordon so much it hurts. If I let myself think there's hope, it will kill me."

"Well, I'd say your lifespan is going to be pretty short if you keep trying to stay so busy that you can't think. You might as well live dangerously and go for it."

This brought a hysterical kind of chuckle from Charlotte. She stood up and hugged her mom. "I love you and hate you all at the same time. I always have, you know."

"I know. It's a mother's lot in life."

"Thanks for being mine." The two women clung to each other for quite a while.

CHAPTER TWENTY FIVE

Charlotte packed her many bags and returned to Crispens Point. No sooner had she arrived home than her mother called to say that Lyla had gone into early labor and had a little girl, named Margaret, Maggie for short. "Oh, that's wonderful. I should have stayed longer. Should I come back? I want to see her. What does she look like?"

"She's so tiny, just five and a half pounds, but healthy as can be. She has lots of dark hair that sticks out all over. You'd love her. But no, take care of things there first. You'll have plenty of time to see Maggie. She'll be with us for a while. I told Lyla they could stay here until she goes back to work."

"All right. Tell Lyla I love her, and I'm so happy for her."

"I will. I love you."

"I love you too, Mom."

Now that she was home, she wasn't sure where to start, but she thought she'd start at the beginning. She went to Bible study since it was Wednesday night. Janice saw her first and threw her arms around her, "The prodigal girl has come home. Welcome back, Charlotte, we missed you."

"Thanks, I missed you too. It's good to be back." She was afraid to look at Pastor Gordon, but she finally got up the courage. He was examining her face carefully, but when she broke into a smile, he felt the sun had come out after a forty days of rain. His heart leapt at the possibilities.

Somehow, they both got through that evening. Charlotte lingered after the other people left. When it was finally only she and Gordon, she approached him. "I'm sorry I was so abrupt the other day when we talked. If the offer's still open, I'd like very much to go to that Italian restaurant."

Gordon looked at her, trying to figure out the change, "Of course the offer's still open. Will Friday night work for you?"

"That would be great."

"I'll pick you up at six o'clock then."

"Sounds good." She turned to go, when she heard him ask, "What made you change your mind, Charlotte?"

She smiled like someone who knew an inside joke. "I've decided to live dangerously."

Gordon raised his eyebrows.

"I'll have to explain more on Friday night."

"Very well. I'll be patient."

Thursday and Friday were good days for Charlotte. She spent them reading, writing, and taking long walks. She felt like she was preparing for a great battle or maybe a marathon. Either way, she needed to build up her strength. While she was out in the yard Friday, Mrs. Bartholomew wandered over. "Did you have a nice time with your mother?"

"Yes, I did. She's great at giving me perspective."

Mrs. Bartholomew nodded as if she knew exactly what she was talking about. "You know, we have to be careful not to miss life's blessings."

Charlotte looked at her confused. What could she be getting at? "That's true."

"Just because one thing doesn't work out, that doesn't mean another thing won't."

"Yes, you're right." She wondered how this woman could seem to know what she was thinking. When she frowned at her, Mrs. Bartholomew threw up her arms. "I just thought you should know that," then she walked back to her house. Mustard leapt so high in the air chasing a butterfly that he landed on his side. So much for cats always landing on their feet.

"I wonder what that was about?" thought Charlotte.

When she went inside, she decided to call Janice. "Hi."

"Hello."

"Have you got a minute?"

"I always have a minute for you, but that doesn’t' mean I won't have a child hanging on my leg as we speak."

Charlotte laughed. "That's okay. Just hang up on me if it gets to be too much. I'll understand."

"So, what's going on?"

"First, I want to apologize for the way I acted in the park the other day."

"No need to. I shouldn't have pried."

"You weren't prying. I just shut you out and it wasn't fair. I don't want to do that anymore." Then she took a deep breath. "I also wanted you to know that I have a date with Gordon tonight."

"No kidding! That's great. I can't believe it. Am I prophetic or what?"

"I don't know, but before you get too excited, I have something else to tell you. Can I come over for a bit?"

"Sure, I'm just about to put Gina down. Why don't you give me half an hour to read our entire library before she goes to sleep?"

"Fair enough. See you then."

At two o'clock in the afternoon on Thursday, Janice heard Charlotte's entire tale. It explained everything.

Charlotte was grateful that being with Janice had taken up most of the day. Telling her was like a practice run so that it wouldn't be so hard to explain to Gordon. She'd just finished getting ready when he knocked on her door. He came in while she gathered together a light jacket and her purse.

In the car they mostly talked about small things, the way first dates go, and Charlotte couldn't help feeling that what she was about to drop on him wasn't fair, but better he know up front. She'd learned that lesson the hard way. When they entered the restaurant, she was relieved that it was a private place that lent itself to quiet conversation. After they ordered, she plunged ahead. "Gordon, I told you that I'd explain why I refused you the first time you asked me on this date."

"Yes, I'm quite curious about that. Quite cloak and dagger, it is." He noticed that she was twirling her hair with her finger.

"I didn't mean to be mysterious; it's just that I knew I'd need a big chunk of time to explain it."

"We've all the time in the world."

Charlotte nodded. "I was engaged to be married last year."

Gordon looked surprised. "Really? I didn't know that."

"I suppose you wouldn't. I believe I only told Janice." She stopped to take a sip of water because her throat was already dry.

"So, you are feeling gun-shy after that experience?"

"Very, but that's not the point, and that's not why I refused you."

"Keep going."

"The reason this man left me was because of something in my past. It wasn't until after our engagement that I told him about it and he couldn't handle it, so he left me for another woman shortly afterwards."

"I see."

"No, you don't. I haven't told you anything yet." Charlotte was rather short. She thought subconsciously that she was making it easy for Gordon to reject her by her behavior. At that moment the waiter brought their food, so they fell silent. After it was set before them, Charlotte suggested, "Why don't we eat a while before I go on."

"Whatever you want." They tried to eat, but the silence that descended was ridiculous. It was impossible to go back to small talk at this point. Finally Charlotte put her fork down and continued. "I was raised in a Christian home. My parents gave me every opportunity to know Christ and walk with him, but when I hit high school, I rebelled in a big way. I didn't want anything to do with church or my parents. All I wanted was to have fun and be popular. I abandoned my childhood friends and did whatever it took to fit in with the crowds at school. We partied on weekends with lots of drugs and alcohol. My poor parents didn't know what to do with me. They tried everything other than tie me up in my room." At this point Charlotte looked so sad that Gordon wondered if she'd be able to go on, but she took a big breath and continued, "I ran with lots of different boys, but one in particular caught my heart. He was very well liked by everyone and when he noticed me, I would have followed him to the ends of the earth."

Gordon knew what was coming next and wished he could plug his ears. "The inevitable happened. I got pregnant. I was just eighteen years old, and I was having a baby. I thought about getting an abortion but because I'd been adopted, I just couldn't do it. I decided to carry the baby and give it away." Charlotte stopped now unable to go on.

Gordon stared at her, unsure what to say. Finally Charlotte picked up the tale again. "Because I was young and foolish, I wanted a closed adoption. I wanted to give that baby away and never think about it again. What happened instead is that I think about her all the time. I'd give anything to be able to see her again. She'd be almost eleven years old now."

They both sat there in silence picking at their food. When Gordon still didn't say anything, Charlotte began joking, "I'll bet this is the most unusual first date you've ever had. You can write it down as the craziest ever. Anyway, I didn't want you to invest a lot in a relationship without knowing the kind of person you're really dating."

Gordon nodded, "You've certainly given me a lot to think about. I have to admit, I never expected you to tell me all this tonight."

"I'm sure Miss Manners would say I did it all wrong. But I did my life all wrong. That's the real problem."

They finished up their dinner, talking about the weather and youth group. Afterwards, they went to see a movie. When it was over, Gordon took Charlotte home. As he was driving away, the phone rang, "Hi, it's me, Janice. I couldn't wait until morning. What happened tonight?"

"Oh, he was very nice and polite. He didn't say much at all. I think I pretty well scared him away for good."

"I'm sorry, Charlotte. I was hoping for better news."

"Me too. Thanks for caring, Janice." She hung up the phone and went to bed.

CHAPTER TWENTY SIX

Pastor Gordon announced Sunday morning that he would be going on a two-week vacation. Charlotte noticed that he avoided her, so she concluded that he was taking this sudden vacation to get away from her. The realization that living dangerously might actually be dangerous came home to her. It would be tough from now on.

Refusing to give into despair, she stayed busy and involved. One of the things that was a pleasure was to see JoAnn graduate. After the ceremony, she gave Charlotte a big hug. Charlotte couldn't help thinking with satisfaction that because God used her in JoAnn's life, JoAnn wouldn't have to go through what Charlotte was going through now. JoAnn planned to go on to school at the local community college and then transfer to a Christian college. She had decided to be a teacher, which amazed all her instructors who pulled their hair out with her the three years before.

Charlotte also took a trip back to her mom's to see Lyla's baby. As she held the sweet little bundle in her arms, tears rolled down her cheeks at what she'd missed. Although she knew that placing her baby for adoption was the right thing for her, it still was a painful fact that she had to work through now and then.

Her mother was a great comfort to her. When Charlotte told about her one and only date with Gordon, her mom rocked her in her arms as she used to do as a child. Sometimes consequences for past actions seemed too much of a punishment. Margaret wished she could take this one for Charlotte. She remembered how she used to cry when she had to discipline Charlotte when she was little. Her emotions were similar now.

When Charlotte got back to Crispens Point, she spent a couple of afternoons with Janice. Janice had not judged her at all for past behavior. Her attitude was that all teenagers are somewhat loopy, and that those girls that didn't get pregnant but had the same behavior perhaps would never change. "The good thing about you, Charlotte, is that you learned from your mistakes. If you hadn't gone through that, you might have continued on your self-destructive course, and who knows where you'd be today."

"You're right about that, Janice. I think about it often. What would I be like? The thought scares me. So for that reason, I'm glad it happened. I grew up overnight and listened to God for the first time in my life." Charlotte bounced Gina on her lap for a minute before the little girl climbed down to investigate a lady bug walking across the floor. "I don't think there's any chance I would have become a writer, either, without such a traumatic turn of events. The pregnancy isolated me from my friends, causing me to retreat to books and writing. I think, perhaps, that I write romances so that I can make the ending come out the way I want to. The way it did with you and Victor."

Janice smiled a sad smile, wishing such happiness could come to her friend. "Well, I don't know what I'd have done without you. Even with a husband and a child, it's not enough. I still need a friend."

"Thank you, Janice. That means a lot."

Charlotte had agreed in January to teach a class on writing at the community college. These many months later she would rather have skipped it, but perhaps it was best to keep her mind occupied. It would only be for six weeks. She supposed she could endure that.

The first week started with a bang. A young man with slicked back hair, blue jeans, and a T-shirt that said, "King of the Hill" shot his hand into the air. "What in the world could you possibly teach us? I mean, you've written a bunch of books and all, but they're all formula, all the same."

"Have you read all my books?"

"No."

"Have you read any of my books?"

The young man hemmed and hawed. "Not exactly, but I know they're all romances."

"Ah. Do you have something you've written that you'd like to share with the class?"

He started to look like a cornered rat. "Not today."

"Do you want to be a writer?"

"Yea. I want to write fantasy. Like Tolkien."

"Worthy man to look up to. Have you had a publisher interested in your work?"

By now, the boy looked like he wanted to melt into the woodwork. "No," he whined. "But I'm just starting."

"Exactly. And it could very well be that someday you will be much better than I am. But right now, I know at least a little more than you do. Will you give me that much?"

"I guess so." He looked disgusted.

"Thank you. You've actually given me a great introduction to this class. You are the writers. I can't make you into one. If you're a writer, you'll want to write. It will be your recreation. You'll love assignments because it will be a chance to stretch and improve your craft. If you don't have an assignment, you'll find another way to write, even if it's only writing a letter.

“You'll wake up at night because you've just thought of an idea that can't wait, so you'll get up and jot it down. You'll wake up in the morning with excitement because you get to put all the words that have been rolling around in your head on paper and transform them into something worth reading.

"If what I'm talking about sounds crazy to you, you're not ready to be a writer. It's not your passion. You'd better look for something else to be passionate about. If what I'm describing makes your heart beat faster because that's exactly how you feel, you're on your way to being a writer and this class will be very useful to you. I'll give you the tools to start down that path."

Looking out at the twenty or so students she had, Charlotte could tell which ones were thrilled to be there. Although they were the minority, her words made them sit a little straighter and lean forward a bit more. Even the Tolkien worshiper responded to her speech. She felt it was a good start.

After class a woman who'd sat at the back came forward to talk to her. She looked about forty years old from the few grey hairs that threatened to take over and the crow’s feet that spread from the corners of her eyes. "I just wanted to tell you that I'm so excited about this class. When you were talking, I felt like jumping up and shouting. My kids are finally in school, so I'm able to get back to my own education. I'd like to have my own newspaper column in the local paper. I know I can't make a living that way, but that's how I'd like to start. Would you help me?"

"I'd love to. That's a very reasonable goal. So often writers want to start with the great American novel or a beat on the *New York Times*. Some are lucky enough to hit that the first time, but it's rare. Most have to start at a far different place. I'd say you have a good chance of seeing your dream come true." By the way the woman smiled you would have thought that Charlotte promised her a trip to Europe.

They set up a time to get together after the next class. She decided that she'd write a sample column a week besides her class assignment, and Charlotte would critique them. When the woman had ten articles, Charlotte would help her write a query letter to the editor that would include Charlotte's recommendation. She left class flying on a cloud and Charlotte felt almost as good. "Don't let me ever forget my blessings, Lord," she whispered as she walked to her car.

When she reached home, Mrs. Bartholomew was waiting on her doorstep with Mustard asleep on her lap. "Is everything okay, Mrs. B?"

"Oh fine. I just wondered if we could order pizza and watch a movie. I'm in a new movie club and I don't like watching them by myself. I ordered *Citizen Kane.* It used to be my favorite, but I haven't seen it for years. Do you know who Rosebud is?"

"No, I don't. Does she have something to do with the movie?"

"Indeed. You'll have to see it to understand."

"You've got my curiosity up. Let me put my stuff away and I'll be right over."

So the two of them wiled the evening away, and Charlotte discovered everything about Rosebud. When she walked across the street to her own house, she counted her blessings once again. Mrs. Bartholomew had become dear to her.

Mrs. Donahue perceived that something was up between Pastor and Charlotte, but she knew it wasn't quite right. She invited Charlotte over to cheer her up. She'd looked so sad on Sunday. "Do you like Chinese?"

"I love it."

"Good. I made a recipe I got from a Chinese student who lived in our home for a while. It's quite authentic and our rule is we have to use chopsticks to eat it. We're getting pretty good at it, so it's fun to humiliate our guests while they try."

"Very funny."

Mrs. Donahue gave Charlotte some vegetables to cut up. "Are you doing all right, Charlotte? You seem a little down."

"Do I? I guess I have been a bit. I've had a lot going on."

"Yes, you've been a busy woman this spring. Is it too much?"

"No, I'd rather stay active. Sitting at home by myself is no good. Too easy to have a pity party."

"Don't I know it; I'm prone to that myself." Mrs. Donahue threw some meat in a skillet, and it hissed like a snake. "Is there anything I can do to help?"

"Having me over for dinner," Charlotte said with a smile.

"I love doing that. Anything else?"

"Not a thing." Charlotte wished she could tell her more. She'd been so lovely to her, but she couldn't lay herself bare one more time. "You've been wonderful to me. I couldn't wish for anything else."

The two of them drifted into a comfortable silence. Mrs. Donahue understood that Charlotte needed her unconditional love right now, so she bestowed it freely. It was her specialty.

The next day Charlotte decided to drop in on Carrie and her mom to see how they were doing. Timmy once more answered the door, but this time he invited her in. "Mom, it's that lady to see you again," he yelled, as if only one woman had ever called on her.

"What lady?" she bellowed, but this time she didn't scare Charlotte. "Oh, it's you," she said as she ran a hand through her hair. It looked like it hadn't seen a comb in a while. "Have a seat."

"Thank you. Is this a bad time to call?"

"No, not at all. Most evenings we just sit around and play cards or watch TV. What can I do for ya?"

"I just wondered how Carrie was."

"She's not here just now because she has a job at the Dairy Crown. But she's doing pretty well. The doctor we went to has helped a lot. He sent her to a dietician and a counselor who's helped her get on the right track. She still has bad days, but the good ones happen more often, so I'm glad."

"That's wonderful. I've felt bad that I threw the problem at you and then disappeared. It's nice to hear that she's doing well."

"Don't feel bad. Who knows what woulda happened if you hadn't showed up at our door step. I won't be findin' fault with you."

"Thank you. That means a lot."

She left there feeling that perhaps she was tying up lose ends in case she'd have to leave. She wasn't planning on it, but it never hurt to be prepared.

CHAPTER TWENTY SEVEN

The second week that Gordon was gone was a little easier for Charlotte. She pictured herself physically turning him over to God, and that helped her a lot. He wasn't hers that she could cling to. She also thought about how perfect God's plan was for her, and if it didn't include Gordon, then that was for the best. She trusted God as she never had before and thanked Him for the peace that He gave her.

Charlotte had learned a while back that when she tried to fight God, it made her miserable. When she yielded to him, she rose victorious no matter what the circumstances. It had taken her most of her life to learn that lesson, but it was deeply ingrained now. Feeling a newfound freedom, she forged ahead with her life. Writing, teaching, and visiting with others, she found fulfillment once again.

The day Gordon came back into town, she heard about it before she saw him. Mrs. Bartholomew came by as soon as Charlotte arrived home from teaching her class. "Someone came by for you today."

"Oh, who's that?" she asked, expecting it to be Misty or one of her junior high age friends.

"The nice looking young pastor from your church."

Charlotte stopped what she was doing and gave Mrs. B. her full attention. "Are you sure?"

"Yep. He knocked for a long time before he left. I thought for a while he was going to stay until you got home."

"Did he leave a message?"

"Nope, just wandered off down the street."

Charlotte realized she was revealing more of her emotions than she wanted to. "He probably just needed to talk about youth group or something."

"Stayed awfully long to talk about youth group."

"Well, thanks for the information. I'm sure it's nothing."

Mrs. Bartholomew nodded, smiling from ear to ear. She trotted back to her house satisfied that she'd delivered one of the most important spy messages of her life.

Charlotte wondered what in the world he could have wanted. She felt sure he'd left to get away from her, but perhaps he felt bad about that and wanted to talk about it. That was most likely it. Oh well, he'd contact her again when he wanted to. She couldn't afford to guess. She waited anxiously all night for a call, but when it never came, she went to bed and slept restlessly. Whatever he wanted, she wished he'd just get it over with.

When she arrived home from work after a long, hard day, the phone rang, "Charlotte?"

"Yes?"

"I'm so glad you're home. I've been trying to reach you. I came by yesterday, but had a meeting last night so couldn't try again until today. Are you free this evening?"

"I guess so."

He noticed her hesitation. "Charlotte, we need to talk. May I come over?"

"I suppose."

"Okay. I'll be there in about fifteen minutes."

She hung up the phone and stared at the clock. She didn't really want him to come. As long as they didn't speak, there was hope. Once he told her his true thoughts, her dreams would be dashed forever. But she knew that was not realistic, so she prayed for strength and waited for his arrival.

He was only a couple minutes late. When she opened the door, he stood there looking like the dignified, handsome man that he was. How could she have thought that he'd be able to love her? "Hi Charlotte. It's good to see you."

He said it so warmly that it made her feel like crying. Why didn't he just blurt it out and get it over with? "Come on in, Pastor."

"Gordon."

"What?"

"Don't call me Pastor. Call me Gordon. I'm just a regular guy."

"Oh. Okay, Gordon."

"First of all, I want to apologize for taking off so soon after we talked." Just as she thought. He wanted to apologize for his behavior.

"That's all right."

"I needed time to think about what you had to say."

"Of course."

"I went up to this cabin that the Coltons own. Just me and God in the woods. It's exactly what I needed. But after about two days there, I knew I needed to do something else. It was so clear I can't believe I didn't think of it right away. Sometimes God has to hit me over the head to get my attention."

Charlotte nodded and smiled for the first time. She knew what that was like, but she couldn't imagine what he was going to say.

"I contacted your mother. I hope you don't mind. I didn't want to get your hopes up if I wasn't successful, so I asked her to keep it a secret." Charlotte eyes got rounder. What could he possibly need to talk to her mother about? "Anyway, I spent the rest of my vacation doing research and I found her."

Charlotte stared at him as if he said he was walking to Iceland. *What in the world is he talking about? Did he find his dream woman? Why is he telling me this?* All she said was, "Found her?"

"Your daughter. I found your little girl."

It's a good thing Charlotte was sitting; otherwise she would have fallen over. Never in a million years did she expect him to say that. "You did?"

"Yes, I even talked to the family. They sounded really nice. I told them that you'd like to see your daughter again, if it was all right with them. They said that she'd been asking a lot of questions about you, and they thought that would be good."

Charlotte's eyes brimmed with tears. "I can't believe you'd spend your vacation looking for my little girl."

Gordon looked at her so tenderly that it physically hurt. "I'd do anything for you, Charlotte," he said, which caused the tears to flow even more.

"I know you would. You're a good man. You'd do anything for anybody."

Suddenly Gordon seemed more alert that Charlotte didn't understand. "No I wouldn't."

"You wouldn't?"

"No. I mean, I'd do a lot for others, but I'd do anything for you." Gordon looked at Charlotte and thought she looked like a little lost lamb.

"But...what about my past?"

"What's past is past. I have to admit that it did bother me a little. After all, I resisted temptation for years. I always thought the woman I'd end up with would have done the same, but I realized how arrogant that was of me."

"Huh?" Charlotte was really confused now, but she got stuck on his words: "the woman I'd end up with." It made her brain all foggy.

"Christ has forgiven me all my sins, and I've been just as rebellious as you have in my own way. But he never rejected me. Even more, he welcomed me into his family.

Besides, he's put a love in my heart for you that I can't deny. Who am I to question him?"

Charlotte sat glued to her chair. She wanted to get up and dance, shout, anything to release the tumultuous emotions that were flying through her. But all she managed was, "Did you say love?"

Gordon blushed and hung his head, making him even more endearing if that was possible, "I'm sorry. I don't have any right to say such a thing. I don't want to rush you, Charlotte. You've never shown any interest in me, but I've grown to love you so much that I don't mind taking the risk. If you want me to walk out right now, I'll be glad to."

This did make her jump up, "Don't you dare! I'd have to follow you weeping all the way to your house." In response to his smile, she added more calmly, "I love you, too, Gordon. I have from the first moment. It was too good to be true. I couldn't stand it if you rejected me, so I avoided you like the plague."

Gordon stood up too, and pulled her too him. "We're going to have a lot of explaining to do to the congregation. We've been engaged one too many times." He chuckled softly as she melted into his arms. She didn't care how much they had to explain. No one would make her feel bad about this.

CHAPTER TWENTY EIGHT

Charlotte called Janice the next day. "You aren't going to believe this. I've got to come tell you something."

"I'll be here...me, Gina, and the books. See you then."

Charlotte fairly flew to Janice's house and bounced in just like Tigger. "What in the world has gotten into you?"

"You won't believe what Gordon did on his vacation."

"Gordon? We're on a first name basis now? What kind of vacation was this?" Janice looked at her suspiciously.

"He asked me to call him that," she said with her nose slightly in the air.

"That sounds promising. Go on." Janice was picking up Charlotte's excitement.

"He found my baby!"

"What?"

"He did. I was on the phone with her parents this morning. I'm going to meet her this weekend. Gordon's coming with me. Her name is Lisa, by the way."

Janice hugged her and bounced with her, "That's great, Charlotte. I'm so happy for you."

"I know. This has been a dream for so long, but I didn't know where to start. She wants to meet me!"

"Of course, she does. Who wouldn't?"

"Oh you. You're awfully good for my ego." Then she bounced some more as if her legs were full of Mexican jumping beans. "But that's not all."

"It's not? You're certainly full of surprises today."

"He loves me."

"Who?"

"Gordon, silly."

Janice stared and blinked. She worried for a minute about Charlotte's mental stability. "How can he love you? He was engaged to another woman two months ago."

"I know. It's a long story. We've been at cross purposes for far too long. We talked about it last night until two o'clock in the morning."

"Without a chaperone, young lady?" Janice grinned. She was thoroughly enjoying herself. It was nice being the calm one in the relationship for once. "Wow, the church is going to have fun with this one."

Charlotte's brow screwed up like a row of dishtowels. "Do you think it will be awful?"

"Amazingly enough, I don't think so. I believe a whole bunch of us have known this for a long time. Only you and Pastor were in the dark."

Charlotte giggled until she almost fell out of the chair. "I can't believe this is happening to me. I feel like Cinderella."

"Well, ma'am, let me tell you. After the ball, Cinderella had to put up with Prince Charming's dirty socks, big belches, and messy habits."

Charlotte threw her arms out as if embracing the world, "I don't care. I'll put up with them all and nothing anyone's going to tell me can dim it a bit."

Janice smiled with affection, "I'm glad. I wouldn't steal a moment of fairy godmother dust from you."

"I do need one honest answer from you."

"You got it. What is it?"

"Would I make a really wretched pastor's wife?"

"My dear, you'd be the best ever. And I mean it."

Charlotte hugged her one more time, "Thanks Janice. You're the greatest."

Saturday couldn't come quickly enough to suit Charlotte. She longed to meet Lisa at last. She hadn't even held her in the hospital because she was afraid that if she looked at her, she'd never be able to let her go. She'd imagined what she looked like a thousand times and wondered if she'd recognize her.

Gordon came at ten o'clock in the morning to pick her up. They were to meet Lisa and her family at noon and it was a two-hour drive. On the way there, they caught up on many months of missed conversations.

They pulled up to a brick Cape Cod home, with green shutters and a red roof. Primroses lined the sidewalk and pansies peeked out of the bushes in the front. Charlotte sat there looking at the house, afraid to move. "Would you like to pray before we go in?" Gordon's voice startled her. She'd been so lost in thought. "Yes, I would."

"God, we pray that you would calm Charlotte's spirit. We know that you have been working in Lisa's heart to prepare her for this meeting. We ask that you give them both the words to communicate to each other now. We trust you with their emotions and pray that this meeting will help them both close and open a new chapter in their lives. Amen." He then reached over to squeeze Charlotte's hand. She held on to it as if they'd been chained together.

"Are you ready?"

She nodded and reached for the door handle. Gordon scooted around the car and linked her arm in his as they walked up to the house. He rang the doorbell, and they waited about twenty seconds until the door slowly opened. A pleasant looking woman peeked out at them. Her hair was graying at the temples, and she wore a maroon colored jumper over a crisp white blouse. When she saw who it was she broke into a smile that transformed her face. Charlotte loved her immediately for being the woman who'd taken her baby when she couldn't herself. "Oh my, you must be Charlotte." Her voice was soft and tender, putting Charlotte at ease.

"Yes, I am. And you're Elizabeth?"

"In person. Won't you come in?" She led them into a living room that was furnished in floral chintz, looking like a garden had sprung up on all the furniture and curtains. A man stood as they walked in, extending his hand, "Hello, I'm Gary. It's nice to meet you."

After they'd all made their introductions, they sat down. Charlotte realized she was twirling her hair, so she let her hand fall to her lap and said, "It's so kind of you to allow me this meeting. It must have been a shock for you to hear from us out of the blue."

"It certainly was a surprise." Elizabeth smoothed her dress as she spoke. "But after the initial shock wore off, I knew it was perfect timing. Lisa has known since she was very young that she was adopted, but not until the last few months had she shown any curiosity about you. When Gordon called, I knew the time was right."

"I suppose you thought that with a closed adoption you'd never have to deal with me."

"Not at all. It bothered me a lot that you wanted it to be closed. I felt sure you'd change your mind sometime."

"I've wanted to see her for years, but I didn't know where to start to find her. Now I realize the time is perfect. A few years ago may have been all wrong."

Gary had been silent but now spoke up, "Lisa spent the night with a friend last night. She's supposed to be home any time now. We'd hoped she'd be here by the time you got here."

"Yes, can I get you some iced tea?"

"I'd love some." Gordon's first words showed his enthusiasm and nervousness.

Elizabeth had just disappeared into the kitchen, when the front door flew open with a young girl laughing and waving to someone in a car. "Thanks. I had a great time." She dropped the bag she'd carried and turned around. When she saw Charlotte her mouth dropped open and she stared. Charlotte was speechless as well. Lisa was a miniature version of her at that age. Now that she was in front of her, she had no idea what to say. Fortunately

Gary intervened, "Hi honey, this is Charlotte, as I'm sure you've figured out." He ignored Gordon for now, knowing Charlotte would be the one Lisa cared about.

Charlotte stood up, wanting more than anything to hug Lisa, but waited for her to make the first move. Lisa finally closed her mouth, walked over to Charlotte and shook her hand, "Pleased to meet you." Charlotte grinned at this polite response. Obviously she'd been taught well. It wasn't a hug, but it would have to do. "And I am very pleased to meet you."

Elizabeth walked back into the room with the iced tea. "Oh, hi Lisa. How was your sleep over?"

"It was great, Mom. We had the best time. Jeannie made us play this cool scavenger hunt game. Our team won because we found the most stuff."

Charlotte felt a slight twinge of remorse at this exchange, knowing she'd missed the joys of these daily interactions, but she refused to dwell on that now. Elizabeth turned to her, "Why don't we eat lunch? I've got sandwiches prepared."

They went into the dining room and settled into different chairs. Lisa sat across from Charlotte, "I can't believe how much I look like you. And you're pretty! When I get these braces off I'll be that pretty, won't I Mom?"

Gary grinned, "You'd better be after what those things cost."

Elizabeth gave him a frown. "Of course, you will be."

Lisa ignored them both, "So, what are you like? Are you going to marry this guy?"

Gordon leaned over, "She is. She just doesn't know it yet." Charlotte blushed and Gary guffawed loudly.

Lisa smiled, "Do you have a job?"

"I'm a writer."

"Like for a newspaper or something?"

"No, I write novels."

"Wow, are you famous?"

"Not at all," Charlotte assured her. "Only among a few of my fans."

Lisa looked a little disappointed at that but soon recovered. "Will you give me some of your books to read?"

"As many as you want." This pleased Charlotte more than anything else. She only hoped Lisa would like the books. "Do you like to read?"

At this all three of them burst out laughing. Gary spoke first. "We can hardly get her nose out of a book. Our library has to add on to keep up with her."

"Oh Dad," Lisa waved her hand at him. "They were going to build on anyway."

They continued on with small talk through lunch and then Charlotte helped clean up. While they were washing the dishes, Lisa asked, "So why did you give me up?"

Elizabeth froze, "Lisa!"

"No, no. I want to answer that. I expected her to ask." Charlotte placed the dishtowel down. "I was only eighteen years old when I had you. I didn't love the man who got me pregnant and knew we didn't have a life together. I wanted you to have more, and I see now that I made the right decision." Elizabeth gave her a worried smile.

"We're you real wild in high school?"

Charlotte hated this part of the story. "I guess so. I'm ashamed of it now. I broke my parent's hearts and messed my own life up for quite a long time. I learned all my lessons the hard way. But God is good, and He gave me a whole new start. I have a great life now."

Lisa seemed satisfied with this answer, and they continued to chat about smaller things. She particularly was excited to hear that Charlotte had been adopted too. They talked about all the things they had in common.

When it was time for them to leave, Lisa asked, "Can I come visit her sometime, Mom?"

"Sure, honey. We'll work out a time this summer."

"I'd like that."

"I'd like that too," Charlotte agreed. As she started to walk out the door, Lisa yelled, "Wait." She ran up to Charlotte and threw her arms around her. The tears that Charlotte had been holding back flowed freely now.

In the car, Gordon said, "I don't see how that could have gone any better."

"I don't either. It surpassed my best imaginations."

"It was fun for me. Being around Lisa was like getting to see you as a little girl. I couldn't believe how much she looked like you."

"She truly did," Charlotte laughed. "I could hardly believe it myself."

They sunk into an easy silence. After driving a while, Gordon pulled off at a scenic spot. "Let's get out and stretch for a minute."

Charlotte climbed out and Gordon said, "Look, there's a little creek flowing though the trees. Why don't we walk in there?"

Holding hands they followed the creek for quite a while, startling a muskrat and scaring some geese away. "Now that we've gotten rid of the crowd," Gordon joked, "I can tell you why I brought you here." He took both her hands and looked into her eyes so tenderly that Charlotte's knees felt weak. "I know this is sudden, but I meant what I said back at the house. There's no one else for me but you. Will you marry me?"

Charlotte threw her arms around him, "Of course I will. I don't see how I could live without you."

Gordon smiled and kissed her for the first time. As she melted into his arms, she felt certain that all the creatures of the wood fell silent.

The church took the news pretty well. There were a few that thought the Pastor was a bit flighty with his marriage proposals, but on the whole everyone liked Charlotte so much that they accepted it quite nicely. They told the Donahues first. "I knew it. I knew it. Didn't I tell you right away that they were right for each other?" She looked at her husband with superiority.

"You did indeed, and I thought you were batty. But I'll concede when I'm wrong. I couldn't be happier for you both," and he extended his hand to shake with Pastor, then gave Charlotte a hug.

When their son, Mort, found out his only comment was, "I didn't know romance writers got married!" In response, Gordon good naturedly wrestled him to the ground.

Charlotte made a point to tell Mrs. Bartholomew right away. "Well, it's about time," she declared. "I was afraid that Mustard and I would have to hit you over the head or something."

"What do you mean?"

"Why, I knew from the very beginning that you were in love with him. Every time I mentioned him, you got all moony like. I couldn't understand what was keeping you two apart."

"But it takes two, you know."

"Exactly. He was just as in love with you as you were with him."

Charlotte put her hands on her hips. "Now, how could you possibly know that?"

"Well, my first tip-off was when the young pastor spent that tornado outside your house in the bushes."

"What?" Charlotte looked as shocked as if she'd told her that leprechauns popped out of the ground.

"Yep. That whole storm he was there. I couldn't figure it out other than he wanted to be near you."

Charlotte's eyes teared up again. She was tired of crying, but she couldn't seem to stop the tears of joy. It felt like a time of rain after a long drought. Fortunately Mrs. B continued as if nothing had happened, "The bad thing is that you won't be my neighbor anymore. I'll miss you something fierce."

Charlotte put her arms around her, "I'll only be a few blocks away. You and Mustard and welcome anytime."

She hugged her back, not wanting to let go, "You've been the best neighbor ever. I don't know what we would have done without you."

The wedding day came a few months later. Charlotte's mother was there with her blond-tinted wig, as well as Lyla and her baby. When Lyla heard the news she said, "Hey, there's hope for me. Some stories do have happy endings."

Mrs. Bartholomew was there with Mustard. He had a new collar in honor of the celebration. Misty and her friends as well as all the high school girls helped serve at the reception.

Janice was her matron of honor and Lisa her bridesmaid. She'd been to Charlotte's home three different weekends since their first meeting. They got along like long lost friends. The church had a little more trouble accepting Lisa, but soon her sparkling personality won them over. Charlotte's work with the teenagers had more power as she warned them about the pain of rebelliousness.

When Gordon saw Charlotte walking down the aisle toward him, his heart leapt back to the moment a few months before when he saw her walking down this same aisle. He could hardly believe that this time, he was the groom. As they turned to make their sacred vows in front of these many witnesses, he thought she was the purest, sweetest woman he'd ever seen.

ABOUT THE AUTHOR

JoHannah Reardon is the managing editor of ChristianBibleStudies.com, an online Christianity Today Bible study site.

JoHannah Reardon blogs at johannahreardon.com. If you enjoyed this book, please give it a positive review. Also, check out her other books:

Christian Fiction: Cherry Cobbler, Redbud Corner, Gathering Bittersweet, Journey to Omwana, Prince Crossing
Children's Fiction: The Crumbling Brick
Family Devotional: Proverbs for Kids

Following is a preview of *Cherry Cobbler:*

"Where's Papa going with that ax?" That's how the book *Charlotte's Web* begins. You know the story where the spider saves Wilbur the pig from becoming bacon. I used to cry whenever I read that book as a child. Every time the pig cried, I cried too. Maybe it was because I was rather plump myself and identified too strongly with the main character.

At any rate, that's kind of how I feel now. Just like Wilbur, blubbering because he's about to become someone's breakfast. Not that I'm physically in danger. Not at all. I'm plugging away quite well as far as that goes. No threats on my life, no fatal diseases. In fact, I escaped without even a cold when everyone else called in sick to work. No, my problems are more of the social nature.

Now don't get me wrong. I'm a likeable individual with lots of friends, always the first person to get invited to a party. I often end up in the middle of the room with a crowd gathered around as I tell jokes and generally keep everyone from giving up and going home. Some of my friends plan their parties around me the way they'd plan around a magician or singer they'd invited. So my problem is not being popular. I really am. The trouble is that I'm getting to an age where I want to settle down. I'm twenty-eight years old. If you are any older than that, I'm sure you think I'm quite young. If you are under nineteen, it probably sounds close to death. I don't feel young or close to death, just tired of the carefree single life. There's nothing I'd like more than staying home with my man for a video and some popcorn.

Okay, now it's out. It's the man part I'm missing. I know. These days women are supposed to be independent. They're not supposed to need men. At least that's the message I got as I slugged my way through college. But you know what? Even if we don't need them, they're kind of nice to have around. There are moments at work where I'd trade seven emotional females for one levelheaded male.

I work as a secretary at a garden center. Excuse me, as an administrative assistant. I think everyone gives workers fancy titles these days so they won't have to give them a raise. At least that's what my mom says. When I told her I'd been hired as an administrative assistant, I said it all hoity-toity like it was something important, but she said, "Hrmph. Your dad and I worked all those years to put you through college so you could be a secretary?" Fancy titles never fool Mom.

I went to college to be a teacher. It sounded nice; put together exceptionally motivating lesson plans, give the kids lots of hugs, be a hero. Yea right! I just about got killed during student teaching. Those kids saw right through me. I don't know what I was thinking. I never even liked babysitting.

So after graduating, I stuck my teaching certificate in a drawer and haven't seen it since. I got a job at the garden center. I'd pulled weeds at during college to make some extra cash. They liked me there and I could still hang around my college buddies. But now most of them are gone and I'm still here, looking for more meaning than filing forms and making phone calls.

The good part about staying around is that I stayed involved in my church. I'm from a small town originally, so when I first went to Faith Church, I thought I'd died and gone to heaven. There were people galore, great music, a bazillion programs, and lots of eligible college men running around. I felt certain that I'd find The One at any turn. Ten years later, that idea is growing a little thin.

Don't misunderstand me. I still love Faith Church. I go to a Bible study every week, show up at every women's event the church sponsors, and faithfully attend anything that has to do with food, always my weakness. I even volunteer in the nursery once in a while, which gives credence to the verse that says "I can do everything through him who gives me strength." But the amount of available men has dwindled considerably. Those college men look like my kid brother to me and the older men, like my dad. The only men in my age range who aren't tied down have been married several times already, or are spending most of their evenings at Alcoholics Anonymous. I'm glad they're at church, but I try not to spend too much time talking to them.

Not that they notice me either. I'm not bad looking. I have dark brown hair that used to be shoulder length but is now cut short in what my mom used to call a pixie cut. I still battle my weight although I'm not huge. Size sixteen is only slightly above average from everything I've read. I'm not too tall, in fact I'm kind of on the short side, which I've traditionally blamed my weight on. You know, I don't weigh too much; I'm just not tall enough. I try to keep up on the latest fashions although I've got to admit I've gotten behind a bit on that lately. So why don't they notice me? I've asked myself that question for years.

Do you know I haven't had even one real boyfriend? Well, unless you count Jordan in seventh and eighth grade. Those years were glorious for me. When everyone else was getting braces and glasses, I suddenly slimmed down for about eighteen months and blossomed. The trouble was, I didn't quit blossoming in ninth grade and I outsized Jordan by a good bit. That's when I became a size sixteen. I guess I could be proud of the fact that I'm the same size as when I was fourteen. Not too many women can say that. The odds have to work in my favor sometime.

There are occasions when I get frustrated about my standards. I decided years ago, that I would only marry a man who loved God with all his heart. It really wasn't too hard a decision to make. After all, it wasn't like I was turning down men left and right. Our youth pastor talked about how important it was that we marry someone like-minded on the subject of God, and the one thing I knew was that I loved God. So I began to eliminate potential mates right there and then. And do you know what? I eliminated them all! I couldn't find one guy who loved God as much as I did, until I went to college. Then there were plenty at Faith Church, but no one asked me out. I fell in love at least three times and none of those guys even knew I existed, which probably calls into question the nature of my love. Anyway, I adjusted to this state of affairs pretty well for the last ten years until Todd started coming to the Bible study I attend.

Todd fits my profile of the perfect man. He's thirty-two, 5'10", sandy brown hair, large, rugged build, and spent the last ten years as a missionary to Nigeria. How cool is that! He returned from the mission field because he was lonely and tired and needed a break. Well, I know someone that can help at least the first part of that problem!

So why, do you ask, am I so blue? Because Todd has never been more than polite to me and I've already decided that I want to marry him and help him reach Africa for Christ! Oh man, it's going to be a tough Bible study from now on.

Oh, one other thing. My name is Cherry. Now why would a parent do a thing like that?

Made in the USA
Lexington, KY
06 May 2012